BLOOD AND BUCKSHOT

A hard man, Bart Baxter had carved himself the biggest cattle ranch in the territory from the raw wilderness. If folks objected to his methods he either ignored them or rode rough-shod over them. Nesters accused by his sons of cattle rustling or horse stealing were strung up without a hearing. But when Baxter's men stretched the neck of Handly, a small-time horse breeder, it proved to be one man too many. Now there would be hell to pay!

ED HUNTER

BLOOD AND BUCKSHOT

Complete and Unabridged

LINFORD
Leicester

First published in Great Britain in 1999 by
Robert Hale Limited
London

First Linford Edition
published 2000
by arrangement with
Robert Hale Limited
London

British Library CIP Data

Hunter, Ed
    Blood and buckshot.—Large print ed.—
Linford western library
    1. Western stories
    2. Large type books
    I. Title
    823.9'14 [F]

ISBN 0–7089–5744–7

Published by
F. A. Thorpe (Publishing)
Anstey, Leicestershire

Set by Words & Graphics Ltd.
Anstey, Leicestershire
Printed and bound in Great Britain by
T. J. International Ltd., Padstow, Cornwall

This book is printed on acid-free paper

1

After a night's hell-raising in the town, Hank Baxter waited in the shade of the unpainted shack on the Handly place. He had been there watching the well since long before sun-up. At last, he heard the door creak open; this was soon followed by the unmistakable rattle of a pail handle, then heavy boots approached, crunching gravel.

In the light of the early morning sun, an elongated shadow came into view, heading for the well. He had been right, it was the nester's son who attended to the morning's water for the kitchen.

At the first sound, Hank's mouth had dried like old leather. Taking his half-smoked cigarette he tossed it on the ground and heeled it into the dust. He licked his tobacco-stained lips before wiping sweat from his hands on to the seat of his pants. Easing his guns in their holsters, he swallowed hard, pulled down the brim of his hat to shield his eyes then moved from the shadows and stepped out into the sunlight.

The bucket rattled and splashed in the well to be drawn back up again on a rusting windlass which squeaked, in sore need of grease. Stepping silently as a cat, the hard-eyed ambusher, big as a grizzly and twice as mean, adopted the half-crouching stance of a gunfighter. Eager for action, his hooked fingers hovered tense as wolf-trap springs, a mere inch above his pistol butts.

'You call it, fella,' he voiced suddenly, disrupting the peace of the morning. 'You an me have a settlin' to do.'

The skinny, freckled-faced kid standing by the well twisted round to stand open-mouthed and with his eyes almost popping from his skull. Stepping back a couple of paces, he didn't pay any heed to the water which slopped from the bucket soaking his trouser leg and running down into his boot. He was scared witless and his challenger knew it.

'On the count of three, draw.' The gunman's lips twisted into a sneering grin. 'If ya don't . . . I'll start shootin' bits off ya anyhow, until there ain't nothin' left a dog would look at.'

'I can't . . . I ain't got no gun. You ain't blind, Hank Baxter, you can see. Shootin' an unarmed man, that's against the law. It's just downright murder.'

Baxter's grin broadened some more, clearly enjoying his moment of superiority and the obvious fear on the face of the unarmed youth facing him.

'You know that and I know that, but there ain't nobody else here that does. Anyhow, who says you're a *man*? Besides, the law didn't do much for your daddy. Too bad your old man was too mean to buy ya a gun before he got his neck stretched.'

Faster than the eye could see, Hank Baxter whipped out his Colts and levelled them at the youth. 'Say your prayers, Jimmy boy, you're on your way to meet up with your old man again.' He raised his voice to a shout. 'Go on, do like I said . . . pray!'

Visibly trembling, Jimmy shut his eyes tight and began to gabble the words his mother had taught him from the family Bible.

' 'The Lord is my shepherd I shall not want' . . . ' The pistols cocked ominously, his breathing grew quicker and accelerating heartbeats pounded in his ears like mallets beating on an empty water barrel. Then, as he finished the last line he heard the count begin.'

'One . . . two . . . '

Two gunshots boomed out almost simultaneously from somewhere behind him. Jimmy reacted, jumped like a frog on a hot rock, let the bucket drop from his hand then waited for the surge of pain, but there was none.

When he dared to open his eyes, to his amazement he saw the gunman flat on his back, spreadeagled in the dust a couple of yards further away than he had been. The dead man's features were unrecognizable, having been reduced to a bloody pulp with only one eyeball hanging naked where the left cheek had been.

'You're all right now, Jimmy,' his sister Sarah reassured him. Stepping out from behind the end of the cabin she deftly withdrew both of the still-smoking cartridge cases from an old twelve-gauge shotgun. 'Don't you worry none, little brother, there ain't anyone round here who's goin' to harm a hair on your hide while I'm around.'

'But, Sarah, they will, and you know it As soon as his kin find out that Hank's dead, and that it was you who killed him, all of them murderin' Baxters will be here . . . And they'll string us up the same as they did with Pa, and he did nothin' except to try to be neighbourly.'

'No they won't.' She shook her head

with conviction. 'Not if they don't know for sure that he's dead. And to know that . . . well, they'll have to find him first, won't they?'

'But, Sarah?' he began, unable to prevent tears of relief bursting from between his eyelids.

'There you go again, *but* this an' *but* that. I do declare you've got more buts than an old Billy-goat. Now you stop that blubberin', d'you hear? Go get a spade and dig a grave while I find his horse and attend to that. When I get back we'll go ahead and bury the son-of-a-bitch.'

'Where?'

For a moment or two she looked around, frowning as she considered the problem, then she brightened and pointed with the shotgun. 'I reckon we'll plant him over there, just about three feet inside the gateway of the corral.'

★ ★ ★

Three miles south-west of the homestead, Sarah gave Hank Baxter's chestnut a parting slap on its rump with the end of her reins and watched it gallop away into the scrub. Then she turned her own horse and headed back to rejoin her brother and help to finish their gruesome task.

'I'm sweating like a fresh boiled ham,' she panted, as the midday sun crawled by overhead. Together they used their shovels to pat down the dusty earth on the new grave. He straightened up and wiped at his face with the tail of his shirt.

'When do you reckon that horse'll get back to the Baxter place, Sis?'

Sarah shrugged and administered a final pat with her shovel.

'Who knows? When it's hungry I guess. But that's no guarantee.' Shouldering her implement, she took the one from her brother. 'I'll put these back in the barn. You round up the horses and drive them back into here.'

'For what?' he argued, 'That'll be a complete waste of time, they're all right where they are. If we put them in the corral one of us will have to feed and water them. And I can guess who that's gonna be . . . me!'

She stabbed a finger towards the grave and snapped at him.

'You see that?'

'I ain't blind. Of course I do.'

'Exactly! It stands out like a boil on a new baby's backside. And anyone else who happens to ride by this way is gonna see it too . . . Especially them Baxters, because they'll be lookin'.'

'Rounding up the horses won't stop that, will it, eh?'

'Sometimes, Jimmy, I swear you can be downright pig-headed as well as dumb. Now, go get them loose horses gathered in and run 'em round in this corral. I want their hooves to trample and wipe out any signs of a grave ever havin' been dug here . . . Savvy?'

* * *

8

At the supper-table on the same night, Bart Baxter, the owner of the Double 'B' ranch, stopped eating and looked across at an empty chair for the umpteenth time.

'Now, boys, I want you all t' listen, and listen real good.'

The clatter of cutlery on plates stopped and everything went silent.

'When Hank didn't show for supper and you said he had ridden out like he was goin' t' town last night, I thought he'd just gone to sow a few wild oats maybe, same as any young fella with red blood in his veins. Now to go havin' a fling for one night, even missing a day's work because of it, I can understand.' Pausing he seemed to look back into the distant past and then grinned as he nodded. 'Did the same myself once or twice when I was young and fancy-free . . . but to miss his supper twice because of it, that ain't like Hank. No sir, it dang well ain't.'

'That's right, Pa,' Matt the eldest of the sons agreed. 'Hank's always been

9

more than a mite wild, but he likes his grub and he sure ain't lazy. He always works his stint regular, the same as the rest of us.'

Bart held up his hand as everyone seemed to back Matt up. 'When I ask you all questions I expect answers that mean something. Not for you all to mouth off like a lot of old women at a hoe-down. Now . . . your kid brother ain't sittin' at this table. Who knows the whys an' wherefores?'

All around the table the brothers exchanged glances and shrugged helplessly, but nobody spoke.

'Remember,' the head of the Baxters warned, 'if any of you know somethin' and don't tell me, that's just the same as lyin' in my book. And when anybody lies to me, well . . . ' He clenched both fists and shook them with malice. 'So if ya know, spit it out.' Again his eyes swept around his sons' faces. but only one member of the family showed a slight hint of wanting to speak. Bart raised his eyebrows.

'Yes, Luke, you planning to belch wind, or are you bent on saying somethin'?'

'It was just a thought, Pa.'

'Well, don't act like a blushing bride, we're all full-grown men here. Out with it!'

'Hank's bird-dog, it's still chained up at his kennel. I noticed the cook feeding him some scraps before we came in to supper. Now we all know our Hank, he don't ever go anywhere without that dog unless he's planning on visitin' a real fancy whore-house . . . yes sir, and I mean fancy! If it ain't, the dog goes with him.'

'Yeah, that's right, Luke,' Dale broke in. 'Sometimes I'd swear Hank thinks more of that hound-dog than he does of any one of us.'

'Hey, supposin' he's slapped another whore around,' Matt suggested. 'Remember what the sheriff warned last time?'

Bart Baxter pursed his lips, frowned and pushed back his chair. He stood up and waited a second or two before he came to a conclusion.

'Yeah, that's a reasonable possibility, but that tinbadge sheriff don't worry me none. Right, all of you, get ready to ride, we're goin' into town to look for your brother.'

'But we haven't finished supper,' Matt complained.

'You have now,' his father growled, with all the authority of his years as head of the family. 'Move yer ass. And all of you, make sure you're loaded for bear, in case we hit upon trouble.'

★ ★ ★

The Baxters rode into town in line abreast, neither turning aside or stopping for anyone barring their way. At the sheriff's office they stopped, tied their mounts to the hitching rail and, led by Bart, barged in.

'Where's my boy?' Baxter senior demanded to know. 'If you've got him locked up I want to see him . . . now!'

12

Aghast, the sheriff sat behind his desk and stared grim-mouthed.

'What in hell's name is this, Baxter? What are you talking about?'

'My boy, Hank. He ain't come home like he's supposed to. We reckoned he might have been arrested for somethin' or other.'

'Such as?'

'How the hell should I know? You lawmen seem to lock anybody up for no account at all.'

'Well, your boy isn't here. In fact I ain't laid eyes on him for more than a week.'

Bart turned to his eldest son and jerked his head towards the door to the cells.

'Luke, you take a gander in the cells; check and see if Hank's in there.'

Without any hesitation Luke lifted the bunch of keys from the bent nail in the wall by the door and began to try each one in the lock.

The sheriff lost his cool and stood up as if to stop Luke, but he relented

13

and sat on his chair again when he found himself peering down the barrels of three unwavering revolvers.

'You can't come in here and do this. Just who in tarnation do you think you are, Baxter?'

'I'll tell you exactly who we are.' Bart leaned on the desk and snarled into the sheriff's face. 'We're Baxters, the ones who found this valley, and opened it up for the rest of you Easterners to come in and make an easy livin'. That's who we are. And we're lookin' for my youngest, and we'll find him, no matter what.'

Luke's voice echoed from inside the cell block.

'Hank's not here, Pa. Nobody else is either,' he added, as he came into view and shut the door behind him.

'There,' said the lawman with a smug smile creasing his face. 'You think I make a habit of telling lies, eh?'

'No, Sheriff', Bart spoke quietly now. 'Just any damn time you think a lie favours you, I'd bet big money you will.' With that he turned and stomped out with the three sons following close behind.

They tried the saloons, the barber and the bathhouse, but all with the same result: Hank had not been seen by anyone on the previous night.

'Strange for that boy to miss out the saloons,' Bart commented. 'I ain't ever seen him come from town completely sober.'

'Hank didn't need to go to a saloon, Pa,' Dale pointed out. 'That new whorehouse outside the town has real good liquor.'

'Well, why in tarnation didn't ya say, boy? Don't just stand there like a friggin' fence-post, show us the way.'

The madam was delighted. She opened the door and waved them in.

'Girls, booze or both, we've got them in plenty. Just make yourselves comfortable at the bar and I'll send the girls down to entertain and get to know you before you get down to the real business.'

'We ain't here to try your gals, nor are we in need of whiskey. I'm lookin' for my son. Goes by the name of Hank Baxter. A big, well-made young fella, always dresses in black and wears a matched pair of six-guns.'

'Oh . . . *him*.' The madam's attitude changed abruptly. 'He's nothin' but a whole heap of trouble, that boy. Got himself drunk silly and demanded one of my girls make love with him on the bar-top in front of all the clients.'

'He didn't.' Matt spoke in awe.

'Mister, ask my girls, they'll tell you I ain't lyin'. He tried hard enough, but a few of the boys put him on his horse and sent him home.'

'What time was it?' asked Bart. 'It's important to me.'

'Oh?' Her eyes glittered with avarice and she held her palm out to him. 'And how important is that, may I ask?'

'At a guess I'd say ten dollars.'

'Ah,' she pouted. 'Not so important.

16

Strange how memory goes, just when you need it.'

'All right,' he replied 'Twenty dollars, that's my top bid.'

She beamed a smile and snatched the gold piece.

'Well, what time was it?'

'Shortly after midnight. Believe me, mister, he was as drunk as an alcoholic skunk. I don't know how he sat his horse, but somehow he did. I know because I watched him ride out from here, and it cost me a round of free drinks for the boys who put him in the saddle.'

'Which way was he heading?'

'Mister, you sure expect a lot for a miserly twenty bucks.' She became aware of the sudden steely glint in his eyes. 'East,' she relented sullenly. 'He headed east. Ask my barman if you don't believe me.'

'And he wasn't hurt in any way?'

She shook her head.

'No . . . only his pride.'

* * *

Next morning dawned and Jimmy did the usual chore of going to the well to get water, but this time he came running back with his bucket empty.

'Sis, it's the Baxters! All of them and they're riding this way.'

2

'Hold it . . . stop right where you are!'

Bart Baxter smiled down from his stallion like an indulgent uncle.

'Now that's not a very friendly way to greet folks, is it, little girl?'

'It damn well ain't meant to be. And I ain't no little girl, neither.'

'You sure ain't lyin' there,' Dale chuckled. 'My, how you've growed since we was here last.'

The Baxters all laughed along with him and, following the example of their father, began to dismount.

The shotgun fired once, blasting above their heads like a thunderclap and they all had an immediate change of mind. Luke made to reach for his gun, but she noticed and swung to cover him.

'Don't even think of it, Luke Baxter,'

19

she advised. 'Set one foot on our land and you'll not live long enough to stand on it.' Luke raised himself back into his saddle, and scowled but said nothing. 'You fellas think that because I'm just a female I can't use a scattergun, or any other type of gun for that matter. Well, you're wrong. Make a move and you'll be *dead* wrong.' She waved them away with her twelve-gauge. 'Now, git. We don't want you lynchin' Baxters or any of your kind foulin' up our land.'

'Little girl.' Bart's grin was still on his face, but behind it his teeth were clenched. 'You only have one shell left in that there gun. There are four of us, and we could all plug your hide before you could pull the trigger.'

'Oh yeah?' she smirked, making a deliberate show of aiming straight at his chest. 'If anyone feels lucky and wants to take that chance, you'll be the first to go, Bart Baxter. That, I promise! You and your boys back off . . . now!' She thumbed back the hammer the rest of the way to full cock. 'And I warn ya all, this left barrel is full choke and heavy-loaded for deer.'

Bart Baxter's smile faded, but he still made no move to back away.

'No need to get so dang uppity, I don't mean you no harm, missy. Me and the boys are just passin' through, lookin' for Hank, my youngest. Is he here?' He winked. 'I'm a man of the world. You don't have to worry none, I'll not say a word.' He winked again. 'Us men have to learn about females before we settle on marrying a decent woman.' Leaning towards her, he lowered his tone and spoke confidentially. 'He's in your bedroom maybe?'

'Not on your life.' Sarah's laugh was derisive. 'Surely ya don't think I'd be sparkin' with a fat, no-account drunk like him, do ya? I'd sooner sleep with a hog.'

'My boy ain't no drunk.' Now he no longer concealed his anger. 'He's just a mite playful, likes a little fun, same as most menfolk.' Baxter senior backed his horse and wheeled it to head out.

'Not a drunk?' She carried on taunting, shouting after them as they rode off. 'If he ain't, he's sure been makin' a good try at becomin' one, because I don't know a soul who's ever seen him properly sober.'

When they had ridden out of sight she returned to the house.

'It's all right, Jimmy, they've gone. You can come out now.'

★ ★ ★

That same evening, Matt Baxter, having spent most of the day in the saddle, complained to his father.

'Pa, this don't make sense. We've not seen a sign to say Hank's dead or even in the county. Why don't we go home and have a night's sleep? These horses are plumb worn out. They'll be droppin' dead under us if we don't rest them soon.'

'Yeah, Pa,' Luke backed him. 'Why don't you get the sheriff to telegraph round to all the other lawmen in the state? Get them to keep an eye open for Hank.'

'Yeah, that makes good sense t' me,' Dale butted in. 'That way we'll have more eyes on the lookout for him.'

'You could offer a reward for information. Bet that would get results. Folk'll do anythin' for money.'

'That's not a bad plan, about the telegraph.' Bart admitted, pulling at his moustache and twisting the ends between his finger and thumb. 'Yes, I'll do that . . . but at day-break, we still carry on the search. I want that boy found if it's the last thing any of us does.'

'Hey, how about the dog?' Luke offered, after being struck by a rare wave of inspiration. The rest of them looked at him, waiting for him to say more.

'Well, what about the dog?' Bart snapped. 'Say what you've got to say, but only if it's worth listenin' to, otherwise, shut yer mouth.'

'Let the dog go free in the mornin'.' Luke warmed to the idea and carried on with his theory. 'We could follow it.'

'Hey, that's good thinkin', Brother,' Dale burst out enthusiastically. 'Our Hank was forever boastin' how good that bird-dog was with its nose. He swore blind that hound could back-track a baby gnat's fart in a windstorm.'

Bart, looked through hooded eyes into the distance as he deliberated. After a moment he turned and actually smiled at Dale.

'Boy, you never cease to surprise me. That's a real good bit of thinkin' you've done. You've come up with one hell of an idea.'

★ ★ ★

As she washed the supper dishes, Sarah Handly suddenly stopped, dried her hands and crossed to the table where her kid brother was engrossed in his schooling.

'Jimmy?'

'Uh-huh?'

'Put that book down and listen.'

'Aw heck, first ya tell me I've *got to read*, then when I do, you — '

'Shut up and listen! This is serious.'

'I hate it when you start to talk all that serious stuff . . . it's always supposed to be for my own good, but somehow it sure don't seem like it to me.'

'I think we should move out of this place.'

The book forgotten, Jimmy stared at her with disbelief.

'Move out? You mean . . . go away . . . never come back?'

She nodded

'But why? I like it here.'

'Why! You can ask me that? Jimmy, have ya forgotten what's happened and who we buried out there in the corral?'

'But ya told me it would be safe . . . that the Baxters would never find him. I don't want to go. I like it here.'

'Have you forgotten what they did to our pa, all because a stupid steer from the Double B wandered on to our land and started eatin' our crops? Didn't they accuse him of rustlin' and string him up like he was no more than a side of beef, before our very eyes? With no trial, no nothin'? Remember how they wouldn't listen to us, not even when we got down on our knees and begged them to spare his life?'

'And what did the sheriff do when we went into town to ask for justice?' the boy asked bitterly. 'Nothin', except to say that rustlin' was a hangin' offence and that in his opinion the Baxters had done the state a favour.'

'Well, what do you think the law would say if they happen to find Hank Baxter buried on our land? No, little brother, by my reckoning, we should clear out and start afresh somewhere else.'

'When? Where could we go?'

'The mountains, like Pa was always spoutin' about. I don't see any point in lingering. We can pack what we need right now and be out of here first thing in the mornin'.' Excitement sparkled in her eyes, and she could tell he was catching on to her enthusiasm. 'What ya say to that, little brother?'

'Couldn't we sell the place first?'

Sarah shook her head.

'No, we haven't got time for all that kind of business, it ain't worth much anyhow. We'll take what we can carry with us; any delay could prove to be dangerous. Besides, this is cattle country, who would want to buy a ramshackle cabin sittin' on a skimpy bit of land like this? No, Jimmy, I reckon we should head for the mountains and do what Pa was forever talkin' about doin' but somehow never got round to.'

'Prospectin'? Lookin' for gold; wow, that'll be great,' her brother exclaimed. 'We could be rich. We could buy anythin' we like, just like Pa said.'

Sarah smiled indulgently and ruffled his hair.

'Jimmy, you're a laugh a minute, but still, if we try real hard and happen to be lucky, who knows, we might make a good livin' for ourselves.'

Jimmy lost his grin.

'What about Ma and Pa . . . I mean, how can we take them with us?'

Reaching out she grasped his hand and gave it a squeeze as she explained.

'Jimmy, we can't . . . Besides, they're safe and happy together under that old chestnut tree they liked so much. Nobody's goin' to harm them there.' She sighed as she ruffled his hair again. 'Playtime's over, young fella, it's time for you to get out into that big world out there and grow up to be a man.'

★ ★ ★

An hour after the break of day found them heading north-east and already ten miles from the homestead. Sitting in the driving seat of the bone-rattling ancient flat-top cart, Jimmy urged the team on while his sister, mounted on a dapple-grey mare, expertly wrangled the small remuda of riding horses they had bred on the homestead.

Two days later, tired and trail weary, they trundled into a growing frontier town which appeared to buzz like a beehive on a summer's day They passed under a painted sign which boldly stated that: WORKERS AND BUSINESSMEN ARE WELCOME, BUT SADDLE-TRAMPS, ROWDIES AND TRAILHANDS ARE NOT, BY ORDER OF THE TOWN COMMITTEE.

At the edge of town a huge barn of a building turned out to be a livery stable with room out back in its corral to lodge the remuda for the night. They drove on into town with the cart. They pulled up at a horse trough to let their animals drink when a man in a city suit and wearing an impressive gold watch-chain across his belly waddled over. For a while he stood looking over the flat-top and team, then apparently satisfied, he completely ignored Sarah and spoke directly to Jimmy.

'Where's your old man, son?' he asked brusquely, without removing the cigar from his mouth. 'Does he want to sell this rig and team? I'll pay a fair price.' He waved an arm as though indicating everyone about him. 'Ask anyone and they'll tell you the same.'

'Langford,' a taller and much younger man interjected, as he pushed through the busy throng, 'you wouldn't know a fair price if it came up to you in broad daylight and chewed your leg off. Leave the kid alone, you old buzzard.'

'Why don't you butt out, Craythorn?' The newcomer, dressed smartly in the unmistakable black garb of a professional gambler, flicked his coat back to leave his holstered six-shooter visible and clear for action. His eyes narrowed a little and looked directly into the other man's.

'And who's going to make me?' he asked quietly. 'You?'

'Craythorn, I wouldn't give you the satisfaction,' the fat man sneered, then moved away to mingle with those on the boardwalk as Sarah dismounted from the cart.

'You lookin' for somethin', mister?' she challenged.

The gambler smiled, tweaked his broad-brimmed hat and gave a slight bow.

'Craythorn,' he offered. 'Mark Craythorn, at your service, ma'am.'

'Is that a fact,' she retorted, a hard edge of suspicion in her voice. 'Why?'

'You're strangers here, I wouldn't like to see you robbed on your first day. At least not without me giving you fair warning.'

'We can take care of ourselves,' she informed him in no uncertain terms. 'If we need help we'll ask . . . and Mr Craythorn, we wouldn't ask a gambler.'

'Why not?'

' 'Cos gamblin's a sin, so a fancy-talkin' gambler must be nothin' more than a low-down sinner. Ma and Pa always said that.'

Craythorn raised his eyebrows in

31

feigned surprise at her forthright manner. A smile played on his lips as he turned to the boy.

'Where is your ma and pa, sonny, and why aren't they with you?'

'They're both dead, mister,' Jimmy blurted out.

'Now why did you have to go and tell him that?' Sarah snapped at her brother. 'What we do and where we go ain't nothin' to do with him.'

A ripple of laughter arose from a number of nosy bystanders who had gathered to listen.

'That's where you're wrong, miss.' Pulling the left side of his jacket open, Craythorn revealed a five-pointed silver star pinned to his vest. 'I don't wear this just because it's nice and shiny. I'm the town's elected sheriff. Now, what's your names, where have you come from, and why?'

'We're goin' prospectin',' Jimmy burst out, then added excitedly, 'In the mountains.'

'You hush your tongue, Jimmy

Handly,' his sister warned. 'We ain't out to break no laws, so he has no right to question decent folks like us.'

Craythorn had turned his attention to the load that the cart carried. He untied a rope, pulled aside a tarpaulin sheet and peeked underneath. Again his eyebrows arched and he appeared to be mildly surprised. Turning towards them again he looked from one to another of them, scratched at the side of his face, as if pondering on something.

'Prospecting, you say?' He thumbed back over his shoulder at the load. 'A couple of sides of smoked bacon, that's reasonable, I can understand you hauling that along with you. A sack of beans, and the molasses, I can understand, but the rest of that household junk . . . what are you intending to do with that, furnish a mine?'

This time his eyes focused upon Sarah who attempted to stare back, but instead she quickly flushed and avoided his gaze.

'I asked you a question, miss.'

'Did ya now?' She lifted her nose in the air. 'That don't guarantee that you'll ever get any answer.'

The sheriff sighed and shrugged his shoulders.

'All right, have it your way.' He beckoned with his finger and then indicated the cart to a grinning deputy who had appeared from the crowd on the boardwalk. 'Leave your cart where it is; my deputy will look out for it and see that nothing goes missing. Come along to my office, both of you . . . Now, move your butts!'

3

In a foul mood, Bart Baxter repeatedly walked the polished plank floor of the Double B ranch-house dining-room, his head down and his hands clasped behind his back. At the breakfast-table, his three sons sat quietly anxiously watching and waiting for him to speak.

'I knew it,' Bart declared, stopping suddenly then whirling round to eye them all. 'As soon as Hank's horse came in on its ownsome . . . I thought, my boy's dead. He has to be, or he sure wouldn't be on foot. Ya all know how he always hated walkin' anywhere.'

'Pa,' Dale broke in, 'maybe he's been bush-whacked and just lyin' wounded someplace where we ain't looked yet. It don't say he's dead, just because his stupid horse bolted and wandered back to its stable alone, does it?'

'No, it don't . . . but it sure is a damned good indication that things ain't what they should be,' the ranch owner snapped back.

'We still haven't used the bird-dog properly yet,' Luke chipped in. 'You seemed to think it was a good idea last time I mentioned it. It would be worth a try, wouldn't it?'

'Mm.' The rancher scratched his head. 'Mm, yeah, I did say that, didn't I?' He considered for a while longer before arriving at a conclusion. 'Tell you what ya do: you and Matt ride out with the hound and search every damn nook and cranny between the town and here. Don't miss a place. If that don't work, then you widen the search until it does.'

'Ah heck,' Matt groaned out loud. 'Me and that dog don't get on.'

'That's too bad, but you'd better get used to it,' Bart informed him. 'Because I don't want either one of yer to come back here without your kid brother 'til you've covered every g'damn inch of this ranch. I want my boy here . . . dead or alive. Understand?'

★ ★ ★

Sherrif Craythorn sat at his desk, resting his chin on his knuckles while he perused Jimmy and Sarah Handly who stood unhappily in front of him.

'So you're orphans. And yet you tell me that you own that flat-top cart, the team and everything in its load. You sure don't remind me of any poor orphans I've seen. Are you still sticking to that story?'

'You think we're lyin'?' Sarah burst out. 'Mister, I'll have you know our folks were God-fearin' decent people, and they brought Jimmy an' me up the same as them.'

'All right, keep your shirt on; we'll just have to put it to the test, won't we?' He scribbled for several minutes with a pencil on a sheet of paper. When he had finished he folded the paper and looked towards the deputy

37

who had been leaning his back on the office door while picking his teeth with a match. 'You know what to do with this, Charlie.' He held the paper up so the deputy could see it. Tell them to get a move on. I need to know urgently.'

Craythorn stood up and collected a bunch of keys from his desk drawer, crossed the office and opened a door.

'In here, you two.'

'Thought you told us you weren't arresting us?' Sarah snarled in disgust, when she viewed the three cells in a dreary, almost airless room stinking of the stale sweat of many previous inmates. 'Seems to me that you're the one round here who can't be trusted.'

The cell door clanged shut behind them before the sheriff spoke again.

'You're not arrested, but I'm holding you here until I find out if you're lying or not. For all I know your folks could be out of their minds worrying and wondering where you are. Now, why don't you settle back on the bunks and enjoy the scenery.' Laughing, he locked the iron-barred door. 'Don't bother to ring for room service . . . it's the maid's day off.'

'Hey, Sheriff,' Jimmy yelled. 'Supposin' one of us wants to use the privy?'

'There's a bucket in the corner, isn't there?'

'Ya don't think I'd use a bucket, do you?' Sarah screamed. 'In front of him? It ain't decent!'

'Hold your horses, I was only kidding. If you have a need, call out and one of us will take you outside to the privy. But, mind you, don't push your luck by calling every five minutes.'

Around five o'clock on that same afternoon, a deputy came and unlocked the cell.

'The sheriff wants to speak t' the both of you,' he said, standing aside to let them pass. 'Go on in and see what he wants.'

'What's it this time, you gonna hang us?' Sarah asked sarcastically, as once again she stood in front of the office desk with her brother at her side.

'I could be tempted,' Craythorn grinned. 'Grab yourselves a chair and let's shoot the breeze, I've got some good news for you.'

Sarah looked at her brother and winked as they settled on the seats.

'They're gonna shoot us instead,' she said, loud enough for the lawman to hear. 'I think they want to let out the rooms for rent.'

'I've had a wire back from your local sheriff,' Craythorn announced, ignoring the sarcasm. 'He tells me you're who you say you are. And it's right, you are orphans and now the owners of some property.'

'So we're free to go?' Jimmy burst out.

'Free as the wind, but I'd like to have a little pow-wow with you before you walk out of here.'

'What about?' enquired Sarah as doubtful as always. 'What do you know that we want to listen to, eh?'

40

'You mentioned earlier on that you'd set your minds on prospecting?'

'So?' Sarah was on the defensive once more.

'So, if you don't know what you're doing and go off half-cock, you'll both come to grief in double-quick time. Maybe end up dead, and I don't want that to happen. Deaths cause me a whole heap of paperwork for the county records.'

'We'll be fine; we know all about prospectin', Sheriff,' Jimmy boasted. 'Our pa used to tell us all about it.'

'Did he tell you that it isn't a good idea trying to take a team and flat-top loaded with useless furniture and stuff into the mountains? Hell, boy, the trails are so narrow and rough, it takes a healthy mule all its time to carry a load up there. Have you any money?'

'A few dollars . . . that's all,' Jimmy answered dejectedly.

'If you had a hundred dollars, that still wouldn't be enough to support one of you, let alone two.'

41

Sarah and her brother looked disbelieving, but he carried on.

'To begin with, you'll need a couple of mules, good, healthy ones. And if you don't want to spend months walking your feet off, you'll want riding horses. Then there'll be tools, guns and ammunition. Warm clothes and good strong boots are essential to stop you from frostbite, or even freezing to death. You'll need to raise quite a grubstake, big enough to buy enough food to last you through worse winters than either of you have ever known before.'

Pausing, he looked at the brother and sister and was amazed they hadn't yet hung their heads in disappointment. Compressing his lips into a determined line, he shook his head and took in a deep breath before continuing with his warnings.

'Up there in those mountains you'll come across men who are outcasts, the lowest dregs of civilization. Men who'd think nothing of slitting your throats for a dime or a cigar . . . or just for the hell of it. And . . . ' — he stared at Sarah — 'it gets mighty lonely for men up there in the high country. That makes it doubly dangerous for any woman . . . Especially when she's young and pretty like you. You savvy, miss?'

Sarah flushed to the roots of her hair under his penetrating gaze, but she managed to stare back. When she spoke it was with the clear intention of countering any arguments he could come up with.

'We're not stupid; we know all about that sort of stuff, Sheriff, that's why we came to be in this here town. We aim to sell most of what we have, then buy in the things we're likely to need.'

Craythorn frowned.

'OK, that might get your mules and maybe another sack of flour, a couple of shovels and stuff like that, but that's about all.'

Sarah grinned and gave him a smug look.

'We know that.'

'Well, don't be stupid, forget about heading to the mountains; stay here in town. Get a job as a cook or something, see if —'

'We'll have enough cash after we sell our horses,' Jimmy butted in, in his usual impetuous way.

'Don't be dumb, boy, I already included those two nags with the rest of your stuff on the cart.'

'Mister, don't call my brother dumb,' Sarah bristled. 'Jimmy's right. We do mean to sell our horses . . . the ones we have in the corral at the livery stables.'

'You got more horses . . . at the livery . . . here?'

'Yeah, good ridin' horses, come and have a look if you still think we're lyin'.' With that she got to her feet and moved towards the door. 'Come on, Jimmy, let's go, we can't afford t' waste our time chin-waggin' when there's *important* things t' do.'

'Wait,' the perplexed sheriff called after them, grabbing his hat and hurrying for the door before it closed. 'I'm coming to see those animals.'

★ ★ ★

Matt and Luke Baxter had followed the bird-dog since early morning, and all it had led them to were coveys of quail and a few jack-rabbits. Tired, dusty and saddle sore, the dejected brothers were slumped in their saddles.

'That lousy mutt ain't goin' to find Hank as long as my ass points downward,' Matt grumbled. 'Why the heck did you have to suggest to the old man that it would?'

'Because I thought it was a smart idea. Pa thought it was too. You was there, you heard him say so. There's plenty of time yet, the dog still might find Hank, you never know, do ya? That would sure do us a whole heap of good in Pa's eyes.'

'Yeah, maybe, and it would put Dale's face out of shape. That would sure sicken him.'

45

The questing dog worked with enthusiasm all day long. Never once did it seem to alter its pace and led them relentlessly on. They topped a low ridge and stopped to give their mounts a breather while the hound sniffed around the bushes at the bottom of the slope.

'Want a chaw?' Luke asked, passing a thick twist of tobacco across to Matt. 'Go easy, that baccy's got to last 'til we get back home.'

Matt took the offering in silence and, to the disgust of his brother, bit a chunk off the twist big enough to fill his cheek.

For a while they sat their saddles in silence letting the horses crop the grass at their feet. Down below, Hank's dog went crazy chasing terrified jack-rabbits from cover to cover.

'That dang dog ain't worth shit,' Matt scowled, then spat a stream of fresh tobacco juice without success at a passing bee. 'To my mind he's too one-sided. If it was mine I'd get that useless critter balanced.'

Luke pondered on the statement for a while, then turned with puzzlement creasing his brow.

'Balanced . . . how d'ya mean, Matt? What would ya balance him with?'

'A piece of lead . . . in his left ear.'

'Now just how in the heck would ya do that?'

'With a gun,' Matt said dryly.

'Would it work?'

'You betcha boots.'

The wrinkles faded from Luke's forehead and he suddenly grinned.

'Aw . . . ya was joshin' me.'

Matt roared with laughter and his slower-minded brother joined in. Still chortling, Luke added to Matt's mirth.

'Ah knew ya was joshin' me all the time . . . Ah knowed ya couldn't really balance a big dog like that with a little bit of lead. The mutt would just waggle his head 'til he shook it out.'

Some time later, when the sun was well across the sky and hovered close to the western horizon, they stopped to have another rest. In the middle distance, about a mile away, they could make out the silhouette of a lone homestead.

Matt contemplated the scene for a while.

'I wonder what she's like in bed?'

'Who?'

'That uppity Handly girl. She sure has grown since we hung her old man.'

'Yeah, we bumped into her when I was in town with Pa; it was about a week before Hank went missin'.' Pa raised his hat to her and said 'Good afternoon Miss Handly', just like that . . . but she lifted her nose in the air like she was quality folk and gave us the dead-eye. Pa just laughed; said a filly like that needed a good stallion to settle her down.'

'She's growed up good.'

'You bet yer boots.' Wide-eyed, Luke demonstrated with his hands 'She's got shiny hair reachin' down nearly to her ass, and a body like a ten dollar whore, but twice as pretty.'

'Nice.'

'Nice? I'll say. I'm a-tellin' ya, nobody I know would ever kick her out of bed.' Luke drooled. 'I tell ya, Matt I'd give six months' wages for a night between the blankets with that filly.'

'Maybe ya won't have to pay anythin'. That kid brother of hers won't be any trouble, we can soon manage him. I don't see any reason why the both of us can't spend a mighty pleasant night with her.'

His eyes popping, Luke burst into an enormous grin of anticipation. For near on a minute he stayed like that enjoying his daydream, then his face changed to display concern.

'But what if she don't want to play our sort of game?'

'Oh she'll play all right'

'How d'ya know that?'

Because . . . we'll damn well make her.'

There were no signs of movement anywhere they looked on the holding. Neither was there the smell of an evening meal cooking, or any smoke coming from the stove-pipe chimney.

Matt Baxter filled with apprehension as he crept up to the side of the cabin. The window shutters had been left open wide and hooked back to the walls. Gingerly raising his head above a windowsill he peeped inside.

'Damnation!' Throwing caution aside he stood up, waved and called out, 'Hey, Luke, the dang place is empty. Looks like they've packed up and moved out.'

Once inside the cabin they searched each and every room in turn. Their voices echoed in the emptiness and they spoke in whispers as though in church. Everything had gone except for the beds and already they had been covered with a fine layer of range dust brought in by the wind from outside.

'Damn an' hell,' Luke cursed, his bottom lip jutting out as, like a petulant child, he stomped about the house. 'I wouldn't care but I'd got my feelin's all worked up and right on the boil, just thinkin' of havin' a real high time' with that gal. When I shut my eyes, I could just about smell her. Jesus, what a friggin' let-down.'

'Will ya stop yer belly-achin'? You ain't the only guy who's in sore need of beddin' a woman. I tell you straight, right now even my horse is startin' to look good. Hell, come to think on it, I wouldn't say no to a dead skunk.'

★ ★ ★

The sun shining through the open shutters woke Matt Baxter as he lay in the bedroll he had spread on one of the beds. Sitting up for a second or two he wondered where he was, then he remembered. The Handly place!

A noise similar to a broken-winded horse being strangled came from the other bedroom. Reaching down Matt picked up one of his boots and hammered the heel against the boarded partition wall.

'Luke, for Christ's sake, stop your snorin'!' Neither the shout or the banging made any difference, Luke still slept blissfully on. Grumbling to himself Matt got up from his bed and, dressed only in his long-johns, went to silence his brother.

'Wha . . . wha . . . what's the matter?' Luke, unlike his brother, jerked into life, immediately fully aware of his situation. 'Where's the dog?' Wide awake he looked around. 'He's been sleepin' here beside me all night.' He patted the bedding. 'Kept me warm as a fresh flapjack.'

'If that friggin' dog's gone missin' Pa's gonna go loco. Come on, get yer lazy ass up and help me find it.'

Not bothering to dress or even put their boots on, they ran outside into the bright morning light, both of them whistling and shouting, calling the dog's name.

The dog barked not far away.

There he is,' Matt exclaimed with some relief. 'Look at the crazy mutt . . . diggin' a friggin' great hole in the corral.'

4

Sarah Handly stood next to the auctioneer beside their cartload of goods outside the livery stable's corral. She touched his arm to gain his attention, then leaned closer to be heard above the noisy crowd of hopeful bidders and nosy watchers.

'You will try real hard to get the most cash for our horses and stuff, won't ya, Mr Goldstein?'

'Young lady, I always do my best when I'm talking money.' Goldstein gave her an encouraging pat on the cheek then, helped by his consumptive clerk, he clambered up on to the cart. 'After all.' he went on, 'the more I make for you,' he panted down at her, 'the more I make for myself.'

Jimmy frowned and pulled his sister aside.

'What's the old goat talkin' about . . . more for himself?'

'Exactly that. And you mind your manners an' be more respectful to older folks. If Momma had heard ya speakin' like that about Mr Goldstein, she'd have given ya a thick ear.'

'But they're our horses an' stuff. I don't see why we should pay out to anybody. We could sell it ourselves, so why do it?'

'Because he knows what he's doin'. Didn't you listen to the sheriff? Mr Goldstein knows the goin' rate of things, and I expect he knows all the folk who do the buyin'. You don't think he's sellin' stuff for us just because he's takin' a liking to us, do ye? He's a professional auctioneer, and auctioneers take a small percentage from each sale.'

'But why?'

'That's how they make a living, stupid.' She stopped speaking and her angry frown changed to a sudden smile as she recognized the sheriff pushing his way through the crowd.

Mark Craythorn tipped his hat and

smiled back at her.

'Quite a crowd you've got interested in your horses. You should do well.' He pointed at a tall city type standing beside the corral gate. 'See him? He's a buyer for the US Government. He does nothing but go around buying horses suitable for the army to use.'

'But will he have much money to buy ours?' Jimmy asked the sheriff.

'At times you're real dumb,' his sister interrupted. 'There ain't anyone who's got more money than the government!'

Above the hubbub of the expectant throng, a hand-bell suddenly rang out and the conversations died. The auctioneer, using both arms, ushered the scattered crowd to come in closer.

'That's right folks, don't be shy, gather round and come nice and near so I can spare my tonsils from overstrain.' He glanced at a notebook. 'Ah yes, lot one, This very fine flat-top cart I'm standing on at this very moment.' He stamped a foot hard making the boards resound. 'There, hear that? Excellent!

Sound as a battleship and ten times more useful.' His finger waved above the upturned faces. 'Now . . . which shrewd man or woman among you is going to commence the bidding?' The sale had begun.

★ ★ ★

Bart stood side by side with the rest of the Baxter clan at the head-end of the re-excavated makeshift grave. As if mesmerized he stared down in horror at the remains of his youngest son. For a long time he said nothing, just carried on staring. Then he heaved a sigh of anguish, turned his back to conceal his face and slowly walked a few yards away from the others. After several sniffs and coughs to cover his emotions he set his jaw and faced them again.

'Yeah, you're right; I had hoped you'd be wrong but I should've known better. It's Hank all right . . . though I wouldn't have known him if it wasn't for his clothes and that gunbelt I bought him for his fifteenth birthday. He's always been proud of that.'

'And now there ain't no doubt who did it neither,' Matt snarled. 'Ya want I should go fetch the sheriff, Pa?'

Grim-faced the rancher rounded on the volunteer.

'The sheriff? I don't need any friggin' sheriff. I know who did it and so do the rest of ya. Handly's spawn, it's got to be, there ain't nobody else to point the finger at.'

In silence, his boys stood shuffling their feet, impatiently waiting for his words of command. In trepidation they watched his temper rising as his face blanched. Then, clenching his ham-like fists, he beat the air with them to emphasize the slow and bitter delivery of his words.

'First of all, you boys get your kid brother's body out of that stink-hole . . . Clean him up good and we'll take him home to be buried, next to his momma . . . with dignity. He's goin' to have flowers, a proper full-time preacher an' everything . . . Momma would've wanted that.'

Removing his hat, Bart held it to his chest as he tilted his head back to gaze skywards. Eyeing him, his sons were embarrassed because for the first time in their lives the could see the glitter of tears in his eyes.

'So help me . . . we're gonna hunt them murderin' Handlys down. I don't care how long it takes. When we find 'em we'll string them dirt farmin' nesters on the highest dang tree around, same as we did to their old man.'

Matt, Luke and Dale, stood in silence, no one wanting to volunteer for the job of retrieving the already stinking cadaver from the grave. Their father, replacing his hat, became aware of their reticence; scowling he made the decision for them.

'Damn your cowardly hides, all three of ya get my boy up out of there . . . *Now!*'

★ ★ ★

With the sheriff accompanying them as they walked back from the auction, the Handlys were clearly delighted.

'I ain't ever seen so much money at one time,' Sarah admitted. 'It's like a dream come true.'

'Yeah, it sure is,' Jimmy blurted out as he gave his imagination full rein. 'I'm gonna buy me a Colt and a fancy gunbelt, same as Hank Baxter had.'

'No you ain't,' his sister was quick to correct him. 'This money's for prospectin', not for enjoyin' ourselves with.'

'That ain't fair. By rights half that money's mine. I'm entitled to a gun.'

'No! And that's that.'

'Hey, you two, calm down . . . come off the boil,' the sheriff advised with a grin. 'Your sister's right, son. Money don't stay long when you set out to spend it.' He turned his attention to Sarah. 'At the same time it wouldn't

60

harm none to buy the boy a twelve-gauge, you'll need one if you still intend to go to those mountains.'

'We have a twelve-gauge already,' Sarah pointed out. 'It's old but does the job same as a new one.'

'I don't want a shotgun . . . I want a pistol!' Jimmy stated. 'Shotguns are for old men or girls.'

'Wrong,' the lawman snapped. 'Shotguns are for filling the cooking pot and, used properly, they'll protect you against bear, mountain lions or fools with pistols. A pistol's for killing men; it's difficult to use well and is liable to get you killed if you wear one.' He paused, took Jimmy by the shoulders and gazed into his eyes. He shook him then asked, 'That what you want . . . kill or be killed? You think that's good, eh?'

'No, but . . . '

'But what?'

'You carry a hand gun.'

'It's something I have to do. I'm the sheriff . . . it goes with my job.

61

Sometimes I have to make a stand against crazy guys who think a gun makes them ten feet tall and invincible. Then it's my duty to show them they ain't.'

For a brief moment it appeared that the boy was about to argue against the lawman's logic again, but he saw Sarah's blue eyes flash a warning to him. To ease his frustration, he took an angry kick at a pebble on the dirt road.

'It ain't fair,' he grumbled. 'Me . . . I never get nothin' good.'

★ ★ ★

'What we doin' out here?' Jimmy twisted his face in disgust and groaned as he and the sheriff arrived at a box canyon which had become the town's rubbish dump. 'Is this all we've come for? Ya call this a surprise, lookin' at a pile of stinking garbage?'

'Get down from your horse and quit

your bellyaching,' Craythorn growled as he dismounted. 'And I mean, now . . . before I give you a real surprise by cutting me a switch of that hazel over yonder and giving your backside a whipping.'

'Huh! Ya wouldn't.'

'You willing to make a bet on that, partner?'

For a second or so, the boy attempted to stare the sheriff in the eyes, but suddenly he gave in and slipped down from the saddle. In an attempt to regain his self-esteem he tried grinning.

'Only jokin', that's all, Sheriff.'

'Is that right, son? Well, take a good look . . . do you see me laughing?'

Jimmy flushed scarlet up to his ears, He gnawed his lip then hung his head, thinking before making a grudging reply.

'No.' Self-conscious he scuffed some gravel with his foot. 'I guess it wasn't such a good joke.'

'I won't argue with that,' the lawman

conceded, taking a box of twelve-gauge cartridges from one of his own saddlebags then handing them to the boy. 'Hold that.'

Puzzled, Jimmy watched with interest as Craythorn slipped out the separated barrels and stock of a shotgun from his saddle holster and expertly clicked them together.

'It ain't new,' he explained, taking hold of the cartridges and passing the gun to the awed boy. 'But it's as good as. Maybe when we get back you'll have the sense to remember to thank your sister for it.'

Jimmy, overjoyed to have his own gun at last, played with the weapon. Opening the breech, holding it to his shoulder, swinging it to aim at various targets no one in their right mind would ever shoot at, he did everything but kiss it.

'Aw, gee, Sheriff . . . aw gee!'

Jimmy was only vaguely aware of barrels of the shotgun being grasped and pushed roughly aside. Slap! The open-handed smack across his face caused him to reel.

'What was that for?' he called out in dismay.

'You pointed that gun right at me. Hasn't anyone ever taught you anything about handling guns?' Without waiting for an answer he continued, 'Never, and I do mean never, point a gun at anyone . . . unless you're intending to pull the trigger and kill.'

'But it wasn't loaded, you know that.'

'Jimmy, you listen and hear me good. Guns that are supposed not to be loaded are the most dangerous kind. Because sometimes they are . . . they go off and somebody's life is over.' He snapped his fingers. 'Snuffed out, as simple as that. Other times, people think they're going to be shot, so they draw and shoot first, then you'll be the one doing the dying . . . So don't point guns . . . right?' The reply was slow in coming. 'I said, right!'

'All right, I won't . . . but ya don't

have to worry none, I know how to use a shotgun, any dang fool can shoot one of these.'

'You don't take to learning easy, do you, son?' Stooping, Craythorn picked up an empty bottle then handed two cartridges to the boy to load. When the gun had been loaded he held the bottle ready to throw. 'Let's see if you're as good as you think you are. Get ready.'

The shotgun swung up and fired as the bottle curved high above the dump The bottle continued its flight and did not smash until it landed.

'I'll get it next time; throw another for me will ye, Sheriff?'

The exercise was repeated with the identical result.

'Not such a good shot, are you, son?'

'You do it, then.'

Calmly the sheriff loaded both barrels and motioned to the boy. 'You throw two bottles . . . at the same time.'

'Both bottles shattered in mid air,

only a split second separating the two.

'Wow-ee!' Jimmy's lower jaw sagged in admiration. 'Show me how ya did that, will ya?'

'First of all, this isn't a rifle. You don't close one eye when you're firing one of these things. Keep them both wide open, look at the target all the time, keep the gun moving through it even after you've squeezed the trigger.' He grinned, withdrew the cartridge cases and handed the empty weapon to the eager boy. 'See . . . easy. Now let's see you try again.'

★ ★ ★

Three weeks had slipped by since Hank Baxter's burial at the Double B, and in all of that time the brothers had scoured the area hunting for the Handlys but without positive results.

'Seems they've just vanished like smoke up a chimney, Pa,' Dale remarked to Bart Baxter as they leaned together against the long bar

67

of the Golden Garter saloon. 'But maybe they're set on comin' back, I mean, they ain't sold their place or nothin' have they? Leastways nobody I've spoken to has been approached.'

Bart drained his glass and banged it back on the counter. Wiping his mouth with the back of his hand he shook his head.

'Them Handlys ain't comin' back. They ain't complete fools; they know what they've done. They ain't ever gonna risk their hides comin' back here.'

'Evenin', Mr Baxter,' a voice came from behind. 'We don't see you or your boys in town much these days.'

Bart Baxter barely twisted his head. He would have recognized that grovelling voice anywhere. It could only belong to the town sheriff.

'Oh, it's you. What's your problem?' As he poured himself another four fingers of red-eye he slipped in the verbal knife. 'Up for re-election again?'

'Only being friendly, Mr Baxter,

68

that's all. But now that ya mention it, the election's only a month off. I'd be mighty gratefel to have your support again.'

'I bet ya would.' In a rare moment of charity, the owner of the Double B slid the half-empty bottle towards the embarrassed lawman. 'Pour yourself a shot of red-eye before you have me in tears.' Leaning closer he added, 'By the way, don't suppose you happen to know where the Handlys have gone, do ya?'

The sheriff paused in the act of pouring his free drink. A sly but thoughtful look spread over his long, narrow face.

'The Handlys . . . you mean the nesters, by the side of your range?'

'Well, I sure ain't talkin' about friggin' royalty.'

The sheriff finished pouring his drink, daring to be a little more generous with the spirit than he normally would.

'Yeah, sure. I know a little about them. Why, is that something I can help you with?' He smirked. 'You know how it works . . . you scratch my back and' — his narrow shoulders hunched into a shrug a vulture would have been proud of — 'you scratch mine.'

Bart turned slowly, reached out an arm, dragged the lawman close enough to feel his breath on his face and gave him a cold-eyed stare.

'Sheriff,' he muttered with menace, 'you hold as much as the time of day back from me and I won't scratch yer back . . . I'll break it.'

'I'll tell you any damn thing you want t' know, Mr Baxter, all you have t' do is ask. Honest. Now please, let go, will ya? It don't look good to the folks round here who have the votes.'

Baxter still gripped the front of the sheriff's vest in his fist. Through clenched teeth he snarled, 'Well, I have asked: now, tell me.'

5

Sheriff Craythorn sat in his usual position at the poker table, his back to the wall of the saloon so that he could keep a wary eye on whoever used the doors. Around the table, the regulars did their damnedest to get their own back.

'Beats me why you bothered to take on the job of sheriff,' Pete Daly, the bearded owner of the only newspaper for fifty miles, grimaced. 'I fold,' he sighed, tossing his cards face down on top of the kitty. 'You make more in one evening at this table than you pick up for a month's salary.'

'Guess it's my lucky night, Pete.' Craythorn, his face as composed as a marble statue, leaned forward and poured a generous drink into Pete's empty glass. 'Have a drink and watch somebody else lose.'

71

'Oh yeah,' said the only other man still sitting in for that particular hand. 'I've an idea you won't be taking any cash tonight.' He picked up some chips and held them over the pile in the centre of the green baize table. Perspiration beaded on his shining forehead and there was a slight tremble to his hand. 'I raise you one hundred.'

'What's the matter, Chester, got yourself a big prial?' Out of the corner of his eye the lawman caught a movement and he left off talking as he watched four strangers breast through the swing doors. They stopped there looking around. Slowly he counted out his chips, all the time keeping his eyes on the newcomers.

'For hell's sake, Sheriff, are ya goin' to bet or back out?' Already, Jones, the storekeeper, was reaching for the kitty, his hand hovering ready to draw it all to himself.

Craythorn watched the oldest new-comer speak to the other three by the doorway and as one they made their way towards the gamblers.

'Raise you your hundred and . . . another nine hundred.' Carefully he placed the chips neatly at the side of the others. 'If you want to see me, it's going to cost you.'

'Which of you guys is the tin star around here?' Bart Baxter spoke loud enough for half the saloon to hear. The room quietened. Everyone waited for the reply.

'Who wants him,' Craythorn answered, without any change of expression except for a nod to the player across the table. 'It's your call, Jones.'

'Me . . . I do. The name's Baxter, Bart Baxter. I'm owner of the Double B. Likely you've heard of me.'

'No, but I'll bet a dime to a bucket of dung you have cattle,' Craythorn replied laconically. 'I'm busy at the present time, but I'll get round to you at the end of this game.'

Oblivious of the tense atmosphere around him, the sweat from the storekeeper's brow formed into rivulets and ran freely down over the fat cheeks to drip from his chin and on to his vest. His shaking hand reached for the chips left in front of him and began to count.

Angered, and not used to being ignored, Bart Baxter stepped close to the table, bent down to grab the edge and was about to heave it up and over when a pistol barrel flashed up and jabbed against his right nostril.

'You deaf, mister?' Craythorn asked. 'I said, after this game. Now, if you don't want an extra big hole to breathe through, tell your boys to unbuckle their gunbelts and drop 'em to the floor. And Baxter, that goes for you too.'

'You sure are gonna be sorry you've done this, mister,' Matt warned. 'Pa don't take kindly t' folks who draw on him, and neither do we.'

'Pa . . . want us t' take him?' Dale asked.

'Don't be stupid, do as the man

says,' Bart growled. 'Ya want t' see my friggin' head blown off?'

Suddenly, oblivious of the drama being enacted within his reaching distance, the storekeeper could stand the strain no longer. With a gesture of despair he slammed his cards face up among the chips as the Baxters' gunbelts thumped on to the wooden floor.

'Just take a look at that. Three kings, a ten and a lousy seven. The best hand I've had in a week, and I'm stacking because I know I'll just fall into another one of your traps again, Sheriff.' He stood and pushed his chair back. 'I'm goin' home; I'm losing no more tonight.'

'Too bad.' Mark Craythorn did not gloat, instead he sighed, scraping the kitty towards himself with his free hand. 'I guess this isn't your day, Mr Jones, you should've called . . . you had me beat.'

'Well, I reckon I paid for the right to see,' Jones said, grabbing the sheriff's cards from where they lay on the baize and turning them over for all to see. A series of gasps and exclamations of wonder rippled around the watchers and players alike.

'Mister, ya sure have gall, stakin' that high with a pair of jacks,' Bart admitted grudgingly, even though the pistol barrel still pushed against his nose.

'But you opened,' one of the other players protested in amazement. 'You never drew a single card, it was all bluff!'

A boyish grin displayed the sheriff's white teeth as he scraped back his chair then stood.

'There's nothing in the rules that says I had to try for a stronger hand, is there?' He jerked his head to his deputy who had stood with his back against a roof support. 'Cash my chips in for me, will you, Charlie, and collect up those gunbelts while I see to these . . . gentlemen.'

Withdrawing his gun from Baxter's

nose, he kept the cattleman covered as he nodded to the swing doors.

'You and your boys move out, and don't try any funny stuff; we're all going to walk across the street to my office. Move.'

★ ★ ★

'Sarah?' Jimmy began, as she sorted out some thicker pieces of wood and placed enough on the campfire to last through the night. 'What did it feel like . . . when you shot an' killed Hank Baxter?'

The directness of his question brought her to a halt and she gazed into the flickering flames thinking about it.

'I can't say, because I don't rightly know,' she answered, moving from the fire and spreading her bedroll close to his. 'I never thought about it in that way before. I've just tried to put it out of my mind like some nasty dream, but one thing I do know, I didn't enjoy it and sure wouldn't like to do it again.'

'But would you do it again if ya had to?' he pressed. 'I mean, if ya had no real choice, same as last time?'

'I had plenty of choice last time.'

'But Hank Baxter was gonna shoot me to bits. He told me so. You saw. You heard him.'

'Well?' she teased. 'What would be so bad about that? I could have stood back and watched. You wouldn't have known anythin' about it, 'cos you'd have been as dead as salt beef.'

Jimmy sat up and stared in disbelief at her as she snuggled down under her blankets.

'That's a lousy thing for a sister t' say to a guy. I'd do it, I'd kill for you . . . anytime.'

She laughed at his intensity, then she stretched out her arm and gripped his shoulder.

'Yeah, I know that, and likewise,' she assured him softly. 'You an' me, we're kin, ain't we? Kinfolk stick up for one another and now we've both got guns, we ain't goin' to let anybody push us

Handlys around any more.' Pressing against his shoulder she shoved him down and pulled his blanket back up to his chin. 'Now we've got that all figured out, settle down and get to sleep, I'm tuckered out.'

★ ★ ★

Their route zigzagged so much to counter the steepness of the mountain slopes that to move two miles as the crow flies they had to travel more than ten, and that over the roughest tracks either had encountered before.

Having reached an exceedingly difficult ascent up and over a bank of loose scree, they were on foot. Each step had to be taken with the utmost care for the loose shale easily dislodged to slither and tumble downhill at the slightest provocation, threatening an avalanche.

'Why has gold to be found only in places that are hard t' get to?' Jimmy gasped, hauling on the reins of the reluctant horses while his sister, bringing up the rear, coaxed the more sure-footed mules. 'Is there some law which says we can't have an easy life?'

'If gold was that easy t' find, it wouldn't be worth a dollar a bucketful. Little brother, believe me, you're gonna have a whole lot of work before you can set ya butt on a garden swing and have folks to fetch and carry for ya at the snap of ya fingers.'

At last they reached the safety of firm ground on a narrow plateau between the edge of a deep gorge and a sheer granite cliff which towered more than a thousand feet above them. Resting a while to regain their breath, they let their animals take advantage of the sparse tufts of grass growing there.

Ignoring everything around him, the youth sat with his legs outspread and his back to the cliff, his shoulders hunched and head down as he whittled at a stick with his knife.

Sarah moved to stand close to the edge of the sheer drop, peeked gingerly down at the river so far below, thrilling to the potential danger of her precarious position. Stepping back to safer ground, she breathed deeply, inhaling and enjoying the cool dust-free mountain air. She turned and watched her brother for a while, wondering at his silence.

'Jimmy?' He made no attempt to answer or even turn his head. She called again, this time much louder. 'You stopped talkin' to me, in a huff or somethin', little brother?' Still there was no answer, he simply kept on shaving thick shavings off the stick.

'All right,' she almost exploded, crossing over to let her shadow fall across him. 'What is it, little brother? What's stuck in your craw this time, eh?' Compressing her lips, she folded her arms and waited for him to speak. Only when she lost her patience and her foot started tapping did she add, 'Little brother, I'm waitin' for yer answer.'

'There ya go again,' he yelled suddenly, angrily drawing back his arm and hurling the stick over the precipice.

'Little brother this, little brother that.'
He stood up, moved close and glared
down at her. 'Look at me, I'm taller
than our pa ever was and a dang sight
taller than you. Stop callin' me *little*,
I ain't a kid anymore . . . And don't
call me Jimmy, neither . . . I hate it.'

Taken aback by this unexpected
outburst, Sarah stood open-mouthed
craning her neck. For the first time
she noticed changes in him that she had
missed through day-to-day familiarity.
The deepening of his voice, the hair
sprouting on his top lip and along his
maturing jawline.

Pursing her lips she nodded her
understanding. When she spoke, her
words were not meant to mock, they
were soft and close to a whisper.

'What should I call you then . . . just
Jimmy?'

'No . . . Jim. Only Jim. Nothin'
else.'

'All right, Jim, but can I tell you
something?'

Frowning, suspicious that she was

about to make a joke of it all he gave a cautious nod.

'Uh-huh. What?'

She reached up to stroke his cheek.

'I reckon it's high time you had a shave.'

★ ★ ★

'And that's why we're here,' Bart Baxter said. 'As soon as I heard our town sheriff mention you'd been makin' enquiries about that pair, I knew where t' come to get justice for my boy.'

'Any of you been sworn in as an official officer of the law for this county, Mr Baxter?'

'No.' The rancher, openly showing distrust, turned round and shrugged his shoulders at his grinning sons. 'No, we ain't.'

'Maybe one of you can show me his badge as a federal marshal?'

Baxter leaned heavily with both hands on the front of the desk and peered through half-closed eyes at Craythorn. He moved his face a mite closer to the unperturbed sheriff, then spoke each word with ultra slow delivery.

'Why the hell should I be?'

Craythorn ignored the question and asked another of his own.

'Perhaps you've brought a request, a warrant for me to serve on the Handly kids, all filled in and signed by some law-official with real authority?'

'Warrant? What in the name of hell would I need a friggin' warrant for? Them two Handly kids murdered my boy, didn't they? Holy hell, Sheriff, I'm tellin' ya, even their old man got himself hanged for cattle rustlin'. They've got the same blood runnin' through their veins as he had. They're rotten to the core. With scum like that I don't need no g'damn piece of paper to get my kind of justice.'

'Yeah, you tell him, Pa,' Dale urged from behind him. The others joined in, spurring him on.

Encouraged, angered and already

super-confident in himself, Bart Baxter could not resist a snigger. Raising a hand he gave the desk a resounding slap with his open palm to emphasize his determination in the matter.

'What's more, I'll tell ya this: I don't have t' ask no dude-suited sheriff with a likin' for poker to help me. I'm gonna see this job through myself, and, by the way, that includes my boys.' Again he slapped the desk-top. 'What's more it ain't — ' All at once he stopped in full flow, disconcerted by the sheriff's penetrating stare coupled with the slow shaking of his head.

'Now *I'll* tell you something, Baxter. In my territory, we stick strictly to the letter of the law, so don't get it wrong by thinking you're the king of the castle here. You try having yourself a private manhunt out here, mister. Call my bluff and I'll personally haul each and every one of you baboons in front of the circuit judge.'

'Oh yeah,' Luke sniggered. 'Mister, somehow I don't believe ya know exactly who yer dealin' with?' Proudly he stuck out his chest and then poked at it with his thumb. 'So I'll say it again: we're the *Baxters*. Watch my mouth, fella, and ya might learn somethin you ain't grasped so far. The *Baxters*; a name that counts anywhere. In this country, men stand aside to let us pass by.'

'That's right. You tell 'im, Luke,' Matt burst out in his excitement. 'Pa, tell that guy how we ain't afeared of nothin' he can do, nor that toothless old judge of his neither. Go on, tell him who ya know in the governor's office.'

Bart shut his eyes, grimaced, then rolled his eyeballs to gaze hopefully at the ceiling before making a comment.

'Shut up, stupid,' he growled, without bothering to turn his head. 'Keep friggin' quiet. I'll do my own talkin', so mind yer manners and don't mouth off when I'm jawin' for us all.'

'Now you're talking sense,' Craythorn affirmed, as he looked past the angry rancher to his sons. 'As for that judge you don't seem to think much of . . . he's just an old man. No way near as big and powerful as any one of you, but believe me, he can give an invite to a necktie party you can't refuse. Yes sir, in no time at all he'll have each and everyone of you dancing on the breeze.'

★ ★ ★

Nearing the end of the pass, Jim and Sarah Handly were stiff and sore from the seemingly constant riding. Again they were giving themselves a break by walking and leading their animals on a slack rein. By this time, having left the monotony of the soaring granite cliffs behind, they now found themselves scrambling over or between a jumble of massive rocks left behind by some ancient avalanche.

Having elected to take the point, Jim had drawn abreast one of the larger rocks when the quiet was disrupted by a deep-throated growl. After that everything happened so quickly that neither of them could make a move to prevent it. A lithe and muscular tawny shape launched itself in an arc out from the top of the rock.

'Cougar!' The youth's urgent warning yell rang out even as the mountain lion's expert leap landed it heavily on the shoulders of the horse he had been leading. Helpless because of his inability to retrieve his twelve-gauge from the saddle of the frantic gelding, he shouted again, 'Get ya gun, I can't reach mine . . . shoot the dang thing. Hurry!'

His sister had no need to be told. Already she had attempted to grab her own shotgun from its stowage, but her mount was reacting strongly to the fearful drama so close to her. Apparently as scared as the suffering gelding, the mare jinked and pulled back, making frantic efforts to escape from the scene. Sarah held on to the reins, leaned back against the pull until suddenly the plaited leather bridle seemed to give, squeezed forward past her steed's ears then slipped free over the tossing head.

No longer restricted by her reins, the mare immediately spun round and galloped off to join the mules already making dust back the way they had come.

Deeming the mare to be a lost cause, Sarah dashed to her brother's aid. Neither of them could get near to the horse through fear of being trampled under its iron-shod hooves. The best they could do was snatch up stones to hurl at the cat whenever the opportunity was presented.

Backing, Jim's tortured animal reared up again and again, attempting to dislodge its biting, claw-slashing attacker. But the cougar had survived in the mountains for more than five hard years and knew her business. Gamely she hung on and no amount of bucking would free the grip of her extended claws.

Bleeding, white-eyed, and screaming with terror, the gelding fought for its life. Although yowling and spitting when the occasional well-aimed rock bounced off her hide, the ferocious cat clung like a leech and clamped her salivating jaws on to the arching neck.

By this time, the demented horse had wheeled perilously close to the edge of the rock-strewn trail. Tossing its great head it reared again and, as if to keep its balance, teetered back a step.

'Me-oh-my,' Jim cried out, but could do nothing to prevent the inevitable. 'They're goin' over!'

Although it took only a second for it to occur, to the bystanders the catastrophe seemed to linger for a thousand years. The edge of the precipice broke away under the combined weight of the antagonists. In awe, they watched, open-mouthed, as the animals disappeared from view to be followed by a yard or two of the crumbled edge. The sound of the falling stones bouncing off the side of the gorge on the way down gradually decreased. Then silence, leaving only a small dust cloud drifting until it too dissipated and vanished as though it had never been.

★ ★ ★

None of the Baxter boys so much as whispered a word as they rode with their father on the road out of town. Bart stared ahead, his eyes as fixed as a marble statue's, never appeared to blink. Pockmarked, his face flushed red due to a powerful mixture of anger and acute embarrassment at being made to look a fool in front of his boys. Wrinkling his nose and drawing his lips back from his teeth he muttered to himself

'I hate that dude gambler-cum-sheriff. I'll show him; I'll settle my score with that self-righteous bastard if it's the last thing any of us Baxters do, you see if I friggin' don't.' He raised his voice to the snarl level of a grizzly. 'And I ain't waitin' long to do it.'

'What's that you sayin', Pa?' Luke risked asking. 'Talkin' to me, was ya?'

His brothers cringed at his insensitivity to the situation. They exchanged glances but remained silent.

Slowly, like a lethargic sidewinder considering a strike, Bart twisted round in his saddle. He studied Luke carefully.

Already alarmed, Matt and Dale prudently reined in their horses to drop back a few paces to create space. In their way of thinking it was better that only big-mouthed Luke should catch any bullet if it came to another shooting. With their anxiety mounting, they, like Luke, waited for the explosion.

None came. Instead their father actually smiled at Luke who was so startled by this total lack of rage, he didn't even open his mouth. Instead he sat rigid in his saddle. Bart added a friendly nod to his smile and crooked a finger, coaxing his son to draw closer.

'Come closer, son. I've somethin' to tell ya.'

6

It had taken them more than an hour to back-track, locate and round-up the runaway mare and the mules. Exhausted, Sarah and Jim Handly were glad to be no worse off and returned to the spot where the cougar attack had taken place.

Jim squinted into the last rays of the sun tingeing the rugged mountain tops ahead of them.

'It'll be dark soon,' he pointed out needlessly. 'Better collect some wood and bed down here for the night.' She said nothing but nodded meekly as if glad that the decision had been made for her.

They barely had time to collect enough dead wood to keep a fire going through the night when darkness overtook them. Their so recent experience had taught them a lesson that each would never forget. At all costs they intended to keep a big enough blaze going to scare off any cougar or bear which might happen to prowl near.

'You asleep?' Sarah whispered during the early hours.

'No.'

'Thoughts about that darn cat keepin' ya awake?'

'No, just thinkin', that's all. Makin' up my mind what t' do.'

She sat up in her bed, picked up a stick and poked at the fire to liven it up and give them more light.

'What ya been thinkin' then?'

'I'm goin down after my gun.'

'Down there?' she exclaimed, horrified at the suggestion. 'No, you'll kill yourself. No, Jim, you can forget that, I'll not let you do it; you're not risking your skin for the sake of a second-hand twelve-gauge.'

'You ain't gonna stop me. It's my first gun, we need it and there's no way I'm losin' it.'

True to his word, and in spite of the

endless arguments put up by Sarah, as soon as daylight broke Jim made his preparations. Collecting every length of rope they had brought with them, he tied them into one long line. Satisfied it would hold his weight, he secured one end to a gnarled old tree stump a few feet from where his horse and the cougar had gone over the edge.

'You're a crazy loon . . . ya know that,' his worried sister pointed out as she hugged him hard enough to cause his ribs to creak. 'You be careful now, d'ya hear me, ya dumb ox? Hold on to that rope good an' hard. And remember, you're the only kin I've got.'

Nodding; too emotional to answer in case he changed his mind, Jim grasped the line and looked down over the edge. The amount of rope was nowhere long enough to reach the bottom of the gorge. His only hope was that he could make the rest of the climb unaided. Swallowing hard, he started to sweat for the sight made him feel sick and more than a little dizzy, but although fear seemed about to overwhelm him, his mind was made up. With a show of boyish bravado he flashed a smile at his sister, winked and then carefully lowered his legs over the edge. His feet scrabbled until they found a toe-hold then, hand over hand he sank from her view. He had begun his long descent.

★ ★ ★

Back again in the town that the Baxters had been kicked out of, Luke Baxter enjoyed being popular for once in his life. Having left the others camped ten miles away he alone had ridden back on Bart Baxter's orders and carrying a wad of his money. Following his instructions to the letter, he used the cash as directed, and bought drinks for about half the men in the saloon.

In exchange for these liquid tokens, most of the bar-flies treated him to friendship, slapping his back and acting like he was some long-lost cousin. Most had been ready and willing to gossip, telling him anything they knew or could surmise about the Handly kids.

Rowdy and in full swing, most of the revellers in the saloon showed signs of being the worse for drink when Luke felt a firm tap on his shoulder. Grinning vacantly he turned and focused bleary eyes with some difficulty upon a vaguely familiar face.

'Hi, fella,' he slurred happily. 'Have a drink.'

'I thought it was you,' Craythorn sighed. 'Don't you Baxters understand, are you all too stupid? We don't want your sort in our town.'

Still wearing the same inane grin, swaying unsteadily on his feet and blinking his eyes, Luke waved an arm to indicate his new-found drinking pals.

'These guys do,' he answered smugly, twisting to consult his newly won friends. 'Ain't that right fellas . . . we're all pals here, ain't we, boys?'

A raucous chorus of drunken voices agreed with him but the sheriff paid them no heed. Grasping a handful of Luke's jacket collar he twisted and, almost choking him, heaved him on to his toes.

'Mister, you're under arrest. Walk.' With that, amidst howls of resentment from the freeloaders clutching the remains of their drinks and holding on to the bar, he propelled the bemused Baxter towards the swing doors. 'Where's your old man and your brothers? Are they here in town again?'

Bleary-eyed and lost in his own alcoholic haze of thoughts, Luke valiantly attempted to work out the answer to the question.

'My old man . . . an' my brothers . . . back in town?' He tried to shake his head but instead it wobbled like his neck had been broken.

'Well, are they here or ain't they?'

'Don't know,' Luke giggled, his voice pitched high like a young girl's. 'Pa don't know what I know . . . none of the others do either.' His head wobbled again. 'Ya know, they're always laughin' at me.' He crinkled his eyes and frowned. 'An' ya wouldn't believe it, they treat me like shit.'

'It figures. Can't say as I blame them.'

'Ya know, Sheriff? Pa calls me stupid.' Luke tried to tap the side of his nose mysteriously with his finger but failed and only succeeded at the fourth attempt. 'But I'll show him.' His head wobbled again. 'I'm gonna show 'em all, Sheriff. Yeah, the whole shebang of 'em, you bet yer ass I am.'

★ ★ ★

Worried about the likely outcome if her kid brother should slip, or if the rope snapped during his climb, Sarah strove to keep her mind off such morbid thoughts. Keeping herself busy, she checked and rechecked the packing of the supplies, and also planned a substantial meal for Jim when he returned.

In her anxiety she paid no attention to the antics of the alert mules. If she had, she would have noticed them turn their heads and flick their ears forward to listen. Statue-like, they gazed directly at bushes growing between scattered rocks and boulders further along the trail. And if she had listened carefully she might have heard the occasional scuff of boot-leather on rock. Someone treading softly and slowly was closing in on her.

Every second which passed meant another careful step had brought the unseen stranger that much closer to her. The mare tossed her head, snickered twice and stamped her hooves, but Sarah had long ago become familiar with such sounds, so took no notice and carried on cutting up jerky for the stew.

She settled the wire handle of the billy-can on its improvised hook on a stick over the fire, squatted beside it, stirring until it boiled then put the lid on.

Stepping away from the heat of the fire she collided with someone. Before she had chance to turn or even scream, a man's muscular arm snaked around her waist, crushing her back close to him. A filthy hand clamped over her nose and mouth suffocating her and blocking a scream.

'Quit yer stupid strugglin',' her attacker warned, 'or I'll slit yer friggin' throat.' Unable to breathe she panicked, clawed at and attempted to bite the hand over her face. Lightning quick, his scratched and bleeding hand transferred its grip to her hair, his calloused fingers twisting into the locks and dragging her head back.

Looking up she caught an upside-down view of her attacker's whiskered face. Pock-marked, and with a multitude of blackheads, it housed an evil, twisted mouth full of bad teeth. Cavernous nostrils protruded hair and tunnelled into a hooked nose which clearly had been broken on several previous occasions. Most frightening of all were those cruel dark eyes beneath the heavy brows. Intuition told her that this man was totally without pity.

Foul, tobacco and whiskey-fumed breath engulfed her as he lowered his face closer to hers. When she attempted to recoil, the hand jerked her hair so hard that it nearly snapped her neck, and he growled like an animal.

'Bitch!' His lips drawn back from his teeth hovered barely an inch from her ear and he spoke in a whisper. 'Make a sound, just one . . . ya hear? Don't even fart, or I'll cut ya good. So you remember this . . . I can't abide a noisy woman. One scream, and when I'm done you'll find out what it's like to fly . . . ' Twisting her head round so that she could see the edge of the chasm, he added. 'Over that there cliff.'

He laughed, made a point of scrubbing her cheek with his whiskers and then gave a slobbering kiss between her neck and shoulder.

'No noise,' he reminded her and

pushed his lower body closer to hers. Something hard pressed against her buttocks and she knew it wasn't a gun, She made an effort to pull away but he still held on. 'Yeah, that's old John-Thomas ya can feel. Good an' strong, ain't he?'

Sarah struggled harder this time, but he lifted her off her feet then threw her to the ground and held her as easily as a rangehand downing a calf for branding.

'Always was mighty partial to a young whore,' he explained, as his free hand nonchalantly sent buttons popping as he tore her shirt wide open from neck to waist.

Frantic, Sarah struggled again but her fighting only seemed to inflame him more and give him pleasure. Utilizing his superior weight and strength he pinned her flat on her back. Roughly, his hand toyed with her pert creamy-white breasts, and he drooled.

'These little apples ain't seen much sunshine . . . but they will. Ya might not know it yet, but honey, you're *my* woman now, and you an' me, we's gonna have us a real dandy time.'

Suddenly his eyes narrowed and he glanced round suspiciously.

'What in hell are ya lookin' out there for, gal, you expectin' somebody, eh, is that it?' Yanking her to her feet by her hair he held her body close to his own to act as a shield while forcing her in the direction she had been looking. He came to a halt by the tree stump to stare in dismay at the rope secured to it. More curious than ever he raised a foot and pressed it down on the rope, but it barely budged.

'Well glory be, now what do ya think can be hangin' on the end of this here rope?'

Sarah gave a slight shrug but made no verbal reply. While still retaining his grip on her hair he watched her intently. Stooping he withdrew a knife from a sheath saddle-stitched to the inside of his right boot.

'Heavy,' he muttered, again using his

foot to bounce the rope a number of times. 'But it ain't likely to be anythin' important or why should anyone leave somethin' danglin' like that in midair?' Increasing the twist of his fingers in her hair he forced her to sit beside the tree stump then used the blade to saw at the twisted strands of hemp.

'No!' If it was not her scream, her ashen face would have told him what he had already guessed. 'Please,' she begged, 'don't cut that rope . . . Mister, my kid brother's down there.'

'Oh, now is that a fact? You do surprise me,' he grinned, ceasing his cutting. 'Now that's what I call real sad. But tell me, why would anyone want to do a fool thing like that?' Mocking, he shook his head sadly. 'My, climbin' down a cliff. That boy must be sick in the head.'

In desperation she babbled out and told him of the cougar's unprovoked attack and the trouble it had caused her and Jim. He listened and showed an exaggerated interest.

'Well I'll be,' he nodded. 'Takes guts for any fella to do that, climbin' down a rope, riskin' his neck: and all over a no-account shotgun. Ya think maybe the poor kid's been chawin' on loco weed, or could it be he got himself kicked in the head by one of them fine mules yonder?'

He tapped rhythmically on her head with the flat of his blade.

'Now I wonder, is it likely that brother of yours is on the way back up? Or would ya say the boy is still makin' his way down?'

She merely shut her eyes against the tears.

'Honey, I'm a-talkin' to you. Ah said, what would your opinion be, eh?'

Sarah stayed dumb, unable to put her thoughts into words.

'Ya don't know? Well, we can't blame yer for that, 'cos neither do I,' he said. 'Guess there's only one way for us to be sure.' Using his knife he sawed at the straining rope. 'My guess is he's goin' down.'

'Please . . . no . . . don't do it!'

Her pleading was ignored and the keen-edged blade made short work of its task. With a dull twang, the rope parted leaving the loose end to slither at speed and disappear from their sight over the edge of the abyss.

'Now we both know the way the kid's headin' and it ain't up,' her captor reasoned out loud, slipping his knife back into its hiding place.

Sarah could only gape in horror at where the rope had been.

Jerking her to her feet without pity, he pulled her face close to his own. His foul breath now came in heavy gasps as though he'd run a five mile race. Wide open, his dark eyes stared directly into her own.

'Ya know, darlin', I'm the kind of man . . . who hates uncertainty.'

Moments later, using greater brutal force, he dragged her over beside the campfire and then threw her down as though she meant no more to him than a sack of corn. Tears for her brother continued to burst from tightly shut eyes, then each droplet trickled down her face only to be absorbed by the thirsty earth beneath her head. The worst was about to happen, she was sure of it.

Even when he began to systematically rip off her clothing, she refused to cry out or plead for him to stop. She knew it would be a waste of time to beg, for he was not the merciful type.

His state of excitement grew even greater as more of her pale-skinned body came to light. Spittle frothed on his lips.

If she hoped to see Jimmy avenged, she would obey his killer's every whim. Then, when his guard was down, she would kill him.

7

Jimmy Handly could not make a reasonable guess how long he had been descending. To him, it seemed he'd been suspended between heaven and earth for a lifetime. All he knew was that he wished he hadn't been so big-mouthed and sure of himself. If he had had half the brain of a gopher he would have had the sense to forget the damn gun.

Using the utmost care he climbed hand over hand down the rugged cliff face, resting often, for the rope, not intended for climbing, was a thin one which blistered his skin and cramped his fingers.

Down and down, the descent seemed never ending, until suddenly all of his weight transferred to his hands alone. His feet thrashed about in thin air and could no longer grip or even feel the rope.

Immediately he froze. Then, willing his breathing to come back under his control again, he inhaled deeply and risked a glance down. He discovered that he had underestimated the distance he had lowered himself. To his horror the end of the rope could be clearly seen dangling mere inches above the level of his knees. Tentatively he dared to peer beyond his boots once more.

The sight caused a wave of nausea to sweep over him. There was still a hell of a long way to go before he would reach safety at the bottom of the gorge, much further than he had previously thought.

He was almost tempted to yell for help, but changed his mind when he had decided that would gain nothing. Even if Sarah heard him, there was not a thing she could do to help him out of his present predicament.

Stretching out a leg he used the scuffed toe of his boot to feel for a niche in the rock-face. Finding one, gratefully he pushed his foot into this shallow hollow, rested most of his weight upon it and eased one hand off the rope. Stretching and flexing his skinned and cramped fingers, he luxuriated at being able to gain such welcome if only temporary relief.

The rock moved without warning, then crumbled under Jim's foot. Only just in time his free hand managed to grab on to the rope to take his full weight again. The small section of the cliff face which had broken away now clattered and tumbled into the gorge below where he swung.

With his heart pounding fit to burst, and accompanied by a roaring in his ears, he gasped for breath. Twisting, swinging and bouncing against the cliff face, he ignored his paining hands and the newly inflicted bruises on his knees and elbows. If he wished to survive, hanging on to the rope was all that mattered. However, how long he could sustain his grip he did not know.

It was at that exact moment when he felt a strange vibration being transmitted from the rope to his fingers. He looked upwards. The vibration ceased and the bar-taut hemp rope above suddenly relaxed then snaked and came hurtling towards him.

There was no longer any strain on his hands. No pain or cramp in his fingers. He felt weightless.

The rock face became a blur in front of his eyes and strangely the air moved swiftly up and past him at an alarming rate. Caught by this wind his shirt-tail escaped from his waistband, bared his back and then flapped like a flag about his shoulders. Vaguely he asked himself why? and the answer screamed inside his skull, *Oh God . . . it's me . . . I'm falling!*

★ ★ ★

After spending the night in the cells behind the law office, Luke Baxter awoke with the grandfather of all hangovers. To make things worse, the sheriff turned out to be an early riser and entered the cell block soon after the crack of dawn and gave him a real bawling out.

After this painful period of chastising, he was given an option: either he could go to court and risking having to spend thirty days in the county jail with hard labour and bread and water, or, voluntarily make a donation of twenty dollars cash towards the town's poor and needy.

Because by nature he was inclined to be bone idle, and also because all the money he had on him belonged to his pa, he chose the philanthropic option. Gladly he paid up to help his fellow man.

The sun still kissed the eastern horizon when Mark Craythorn set Luke free. Luke mounted his horse, then without so much as a nod of farewell, rode towards the outskirts of the town. The sheriff waited a few minutes and then being careful to keep out of sight, followed him at a safe distance. Amused at such predictability, the sheriff watched him ride away keeping strictly to the main trail out of town.

After two miles, Luke stopped, checked around then moved off again, this time making a deliberate alteration to his course. Increasing speed he guided his mount along a narrow and overgrown trail.

'Now guess where he's going?' the lawman asked out loud. His horse pricked its ears and flicked them back to listen. Mark merely laughed and slapped the powerful neck with a show of affection. 'Yeah, boy, I reckon you've more between your ears than all them Baxters roped together.'

Close on an hour passed when, some way ahead, wisps of woodsmoke drifted skywards. Luke altered his direction a little, left the trail he had been following, then spurred his mount into a fast canter, making a beeline for the spot.

Content to keep well back and out of sight in case his quarry turned around to check, the sheriff pulled up among a stand of pine. Before dismounting, he opened a saddle-bag, removed a leather-bound telescope and extended it. In no particular hurry, he leaned one shoulder against one of the trees to steady his spyglass as he focused it.

Luke now rode in a direct line between Craythorn and where the pale-blue smoke from a campfire drifted above trees which grew in abundance along the bank of Beaver Creek.

'Well, well,' he muttered to his uninterested horse. 'Seems to me that Baxter and his boys don't rise too early when they're away from home.' With a sharp click he collapsed the telescope and replaced it in his saddle-bag while he continued the one-sided conversation. 'But somehow I think they won't be lingering over their victuals this morning. Not after Luke rides into camp. Then if my hunch is right we'll see them head straight for the mountains. Well, what do you have t' say about that?'

As if understanding every word he uttered, and as though responding to the question, his steed stretched out its majestic head in line with its long neck, curled back his prehensile lips and snickered.

Grinning wider still, at this coincidence, Craythorn patted the animal's shoulder. 'That's my boy. Now you're talking horse sense.'

★ ★ ★

Close by there was an intermittent rustling sound and, added to that, Jimmy heard somebody wheezing as if suffering from a long-established chest problem. He attempted to move, but as soon as he did, pain surged through his body like a flash flood along a creek. Only when his agony had subsided to being bearable did he carefully open his eyes.

Above him, sunlight filtered through

a stretch of dirty old canvas which gently billowed and flapped with each puff of wind. Magically a face appeared and hovered close to his own. It was a white-bearded face with skin the texture and colour of a dried-up walnut. An old face that when it laughed showed it retained only two yellowed fangs and a breath that reeked of rum and the smoke of strong tobacco.

'So you're alive,' the face said, breathing out more fumes and tutting before adding, 'You're one hell of a lucky young fella.'

Jim's eyelids grew too heavy to keep open so he gave in and let them close. He was falling again. Time and time again his terrifying ordeal came back in vivid replays of distorted dreams. In his mind's eye he saw the rope snaking above him. Smashing through bushes growing from out of the cliff face, he repeatedly heard the breaking of branches and then that final terrifying drop through nothingness. His arms and legs waved about, he was afraid as he had never been before and, deep inside him, his soul cried out to express this fear.

The mental pictures always stopped there. After that there was nothing to recall except silence and an empty blackness. And then he had to endure the next nightmare repeat.

The voice persistently faded in and out. At long last it succeeded in breaking through the defences of his mind, battering through the darkness and finally dispersing his hallucinations in bright light.

'Come on, son, take a belt of this.' The neck of a glass bottle pushed in between Jimmy's parched lips to rattle and clink on his teeth.

'No,' he objected, attempting to pull his head away, but the bottle tipped and fiery liquid gushed into his mouth. Automatically he swallowed, but a drop of the fluid went down the wrong way, seeming to burn his throat and causing him to cough violently. He choked and gasped for air, his eyes watered, and he heard the same voice again.

'That's it, you have a real good old cough,' the voice advised. 'Yeah, that's good. Go on, you sick it up, boy, get them poisons an' things clear out of your system.'

Once more the bottle was offered to Jim's lips, but he pursed them and clenched his teeth to bar entry. He turned his face aside, letting the liquid splash on to and sting the grazes on his cheek.

'You're making a mistake, lad, there's nothing quite like a tot of Nelson's Blood to put the life back into a man.'

'Blood?' Jim blurted out. 'Oh my good God,' he gasped, and was sick again.

The old guy cackled. 'It ain't real blood, you young fool, it's a name the sailors give to rum in Her Majesty's Royal Navy. I've drunk it every day since I first took the Queen's shilling. Aye, and that's more than thirty years ago. It ain't done me any harm.' Taking

120

another swig as though to confirm his liking for the spirit, he smacked his lips loudly and winked. 'Jamaica rum; you can't beat it.' Tilting his head, he suddenly grinned. 'Now, shipmate, seeing as how you seem determined to stay alive, and I might not be wastin' my time, let's see what's needed to get you fixed all shipshape and Bristol fashion.'

* * *

'So you see, lad, that's how I came near to being killed twice in the same day.' The old-timer slapped his thigh. 'Once almost being crushed by a horse with a mountain lion on its back and both of 'em trying to fall on me . . . And, blow me down, mate, if later on, *you* don't attempt t' do the self-same bloody thing.' Shaking his head sadly, he added, 'I don't know what to make of it, the world ain't safe any more.'

'Aaah!' Jimmy cried out when the old seadog pulled at his foot to straighten out his leg. 'Hey, take it easy, mister . . . that hurts.'

'Of course it hurts. Broken bones usually do, and believe me, son, you've got more than your share of them.' He made as though to turn away. 'On the other hand, if you ain't ready and man enough to suffer a bit of pain?' Shaking his head he paused, and shrugged. 'Maybe you'd prefer to end up as a cripple and be a beggar, shakin' a tin mug for handouts for the rest of your life.'

He looked for the youth's reactions to the taunts but detected none. Sighing he went on to tell of further consequences which could come about by no treatment.

'Or on the other hand, we could do nothing at all . . . except wait for your flesh to rot and stink like a barracks' latrine in high summer. Then after you've suffered maybe a week or more, you'll die. Gangrene, that's what the sawbones call it, and believe me, shipmate, that ain't a pretty way to go.' He raised an eyebrow. 'Well, is that what you want . . . eh . . . is it?'

The youth bit his lips to hold back his tears as his companion steadfastly gripped his foot and stared into his eyes, challenging him.

'Well, do I mend your bones, or don't I? Personally I don't give a fish's fart either way, so make up your mind.'

'Yeah,' Jim agreed still filled with doubts and fears. 'All right, mister, but please, do me a favour, don't linger over it, will ye?'

'Sensible decision, but stop calling me mister. Sailor, that's what I'm known by and you can call me by it too.' Still holding the foot in one hand he offered the bottle with his other. 'The job's going to take me some time so it's best you swallow down about half of this. You might not like it, but you'll find it'll cut down on the pain.'

'It will?' Doubts showed in the lad's question. 'Ya sure?'

Sailor portrayed the picture of innocence.

'It's my booze . . . would I lie?'

Minutes later, the old sea-dog took back the bottle and without pausing for breath, drained the remainder of the spirit himself.

'Ah, that's better,' he said, oozing satisfaction as he wiped his mouth on the back of his hand. 'Now, me hearty, grit your teeth and hold fast to the rigging. There ain't no use denying it, you're about to pass through stormy seas and this is going t' hurt like your backside's on fire.'

★ ★ ★

Keeping well hidden, Sheriff Mark Craythorn followed the Baxters from the moment they broke camp and headed out. Apparently confident of their own security, they made no attempt to cover their tracks, leaving their trail to be easily read by the lawman on horseback.

By the time the family gang had crossed the last trail he knew his prediction had proved to be correct; they were now riding directly for the mountains and the pass leading to the mine diggings.

'Well,' he said, 'that bunch ain't going prospecting, that's for sure, and they're not wasting any time neither. I'll have to make a move or those two kids' lives won't be worth a rusty fry-pan with a hole in the bottom.'

Leaning forward in the saddle he patted his mount.

'Partner, you and me, we've got ourselves some mighty hard riding to do, and we have to do it now. It can't be helped, we have to make a detour and get ahead of those guys in front.'

Reining off the trail and taking to the rough ground he clicked his tongue. At the same time he nudged the powerful flanks with his heels and the stallion responded by bounding forward with his neck outstretched and its mane flying. With iron-shod hooves thundering in the dust, man and beast sped hell for leather.

Keeping below the skyline, zigzagging through cactus, mesquite and rocks, they travelled in a wide semi-circular detour. At such a pace they quickly drew ahead and were unseen by the Baxters. Finally, well out of sight, Craythorn turned the sweating horse to cut back on to the same trail again, sure that he would reach the pass before the revenge seekers.

★ ★ ★

'Hey, you, what name d' ya go by?'

Sarah walked on aloof and did not reply. Her reward was a swift kick, high in her back between the shoulders, and an instantaneous roar of anger from her captor.

'G'damn it, woman, you answer when I speak t' ya, and be quick about it.' He delivered another kick, she stumbled and would have fallen if he had not pulled hard on the rope which tethered her to his saddle-horn.

126

'You uppity young bitch, you speak when I tell ya or so help me, I'll cut yer friggin' tongue out.'

She realized it would be pointless to suffer his anger. Also she was well aware that he was perfectly capable of carrying out his macabre threat for such an insignificant reason. Choking back the tears, she clenched her teeth and muttered her name.

'What?' he shouted. 'Speak up.'

'Sarah!' The word burst from her and echoed from the mountains.

The rope jerked savagely.

'And I ain't gonna stand for any sassy screamin' neither,' he warned. 'Now you say it again, but properly this time . . . go on, say it.'

'Sarah . . . Sarah Handly.'

'Sarah! Now who in the name of hell and damnation gave ya a stupid name like that?'

'My pa, he had it all picked out for me, even before I was born.'

'Well I don't like it. It's too . . . Bible-like.' His nose wrinkled and his mouth twisted in disapproval. 'Your pa a preacherman?'

'No . . . no he wasn't.'

'Well, I don't give a damn if he was. No, I don't like that name.'

Not caring if he liked her name or not Sarah said nothing, and was glad when he lapsed into silence once more. Not until she had walked more than another mile did he condescend to break the silence again.

'Yeah, Flossie! Now that, that's a good name. Had an old bird-dog bitch by that name once. She never let me down once. Yeah, that's what we'll call ya from now on. Flossie.'

'No you won't,' she flared. 'My name's Sarah. That's how I was baptized, and, mister, that's how I'm gonna stay.'

Once more the rope bit into her flesh as it heaved her close up against the rider's boot. His hand grabbed her hair and shook her until her teeth seemed to rattle like stones in a wooden bucket. When the shaking stopped he spoke again, softly, but with more than a hint of menace.

'It's Flossie . . . understand?' He shook her again. 'Well?'

'Yes,' she agreed tearfully. 'All right.'

'Say it, woman. You tell me what your name is.'

Sarah hesitated but out of the corner of her eye noticed his free hand draw back ready to slap her face. Not wanting to be struck again and for such a poor cause, she blurted out the word he waited for.

'Flossie.'

'And that's your only name. While we're bein' acquainted with names, mine's Nick . . . same as in Old Nick, the Devil.'

'I could've guessed as much,' she burst out. 'And it suits ya.' To her amazement Nick only grinned, pleased by the comparison.

'That's a true observation,' he admitted. 'So don't ya forget it. Do what I say, or I'll send ya straight t' Hell.'

8

Still with her wrists securely tied, Sarah walked alongside her horse while Nick, her tormentor, continued to ride in comfort. Behind them, the mules followed, urged on by frequent cuss-words and tugs on the lead-rope held by the man in the saddle.

After three more miles on the downgrade, the pass ended and divided into two separate trails. The one on the left had a gradual slope and was wide enough for a wagon to use. On the right, the trail appeared to be too narrow, difficult and steep for any vehicle.

Without hesitation Nick took the right-hand fork, yanked at the ropes forcing Sarah and the mules to proceed at a quicker pace down the less hospitable route.

Gradually they were shaded by the

mountain as it came between them and the sun. Before them an undulating valley spread out like a continuous carpet of mottled green. This ended at another range of mountains in the purple-hazed distance.

Still descending, they moved on into the cool gloom of the forest where giant pines, some a hundred feet or more, towered above them. The tightly packed trees kept out the wind noises and most of the daylight. Down at ground level, any rocks still not completely buried under centuries of fallen pine needles were covered in moss and lichens.

Near the bottom of the slope where the ground levelled out, mature trees of ash, oak and maple grew defiantly among the evergreens and the atmosphere grew less sinister.

In a normal state of affairs, Sarah would have been thrilled by such an unusual sight, but circumstances were not normal. In one catastrophic day she had lost her only living kin, everything she possessed had been taken from her, even her virginity. Now with no one to comfort or protect her, she was a captive being dragged along to live or die at the whim of a murderer.

'The boys at the diggin's are sure gonna be appreciative when they see what I've brought back with me. Yes sir, mighty appreciative.' Bending down from the saddle Nick reached out a hand, grabbed her chin and raised it, compelling her to look up at him. 'Woman, ya don't know it yet, but you, you're gonna make me real comfortable. You'll earn me good money and I ain't ever gonna work my ass off again.'

* * *

During that night, a flash of lightning, followed immediately by a tremendous clap of thunder, awoke her from a deep sleep. Within moments heavy rain cascading down through the tree branches above, drenched their shared bedroll and soaked them both to the skin.

'Come on, Flossie, move yer friggin' ass,' Nick yelled at her above the thunderstorm. 'I'll get the horse and mules ready, you be quick an' get packed up. We ain't gonna sleep any more tonight so we might as well move along.'

Rain-soaked strands of hair plastered flat against her face and the newly formed mud squelched under her feet as she scurried about carrying out her allotted task. Shivering and blinking in the torrential downpour, she tensed each time lightning flashes lit the scene as bright as day. She hated thunder and waited filled with apprehension for each rumble to pass on into the distance.

Hardly had they set out on the trail again when a lightning bolt struck an oak, a hundred yards or so ahead of them. In a split second, the strike had cleaved through the trunk of the ancient tree as easy as a sharp axe splitting a dry log of kindling wood.

The stricken oak burst into flame and, in spite of the tremendous deluge, each time curiosity compelled them to turn to look, it still blazed long after they had passed and left it behind.

'Lucky that lightnin' strike didn't start that fire during a dry day,' he yelled at her through the downpour. 'Otherwise we might've been roasted alive before we could get away from here.'

To her surprise when the next flash came she saw he was actually smiling. Slipping his left boot from its stirrup and then leaning over, he held out his hand to her.

'Grab hold and get ya ass up here behind me.' he told her. With that he hauled her up almost before she placed a foot into the stirrup. 'I don't want you too tired to work when we get where we're goin'.'

The glitter and sounds of a river nearby became obvious a short while after they finally rode out from the shade of the trees and into the early morning sunshine. A little further off they could hear the rhythmic ringing notes of distant picks and heavy jack-hammers battering on rock. Nick nodded towards the man-made noises. 'The boys round here get t' work real early,' he explained. 'Seems there ain't never much time to sleep when there's a smell of gold in the air. Gold, it's like a fever. Some men'll catch it and work their guts out just on the off-chance that they'll find it. But if they strike lucky, that's when they really go loco.'

Pausing to shove his hat back and scratch his head a few times he carried on. 'Once a fella's collected a poke or two of dust, he gets t' thinkin' it ain't ever gonna stop comin', and he'll believe he's gonna find twice as much the very next day . . . or the next. That's when they're ready t' spend it on anythin' that takes their fancy. And when they see somethin' they fancy, they'll spend all they've got to get it.'

He laughed out loud and shook his

head. 'Hell, it don't matter what it is. Even if it's just as useless as a worn-out shovel or a fancy vest. If they want it, they'll pay for it, no matter what the cost.'

Nick twisted his head so he could see her face as she sat silently behind him. Smiling again, he told her something which made her mouth turn dry with fear and her pulse to miss a beat.

'And honey, that's where you come in.'

A few hundred yards further on he pulled up the horse on the riverbank and nodded to the swiftly flowing water.

'Go strip off and scrub yourself head to toe as clean as a new bucket. Use some of that fancy stinkin' soap stuff I know you've got tucked away in that there duffel-bag. Fix that hair of yours, and brush it, maybe put a ribbon or somethin' ladylike in it, yeah, and climb into a dress. I want you lookin' real good, an' smellin' just like a woman's supposed to.'

Vaguely through her haze of distress she heard him talk on to explain the next stage in his grand plan.

'When you've prettied up and we ride in to that mining camp, we'll go in real slow. Let them women-hungry miners have plenty of time to feast their eyes on you and recall what they've been amissin' since they left their homes behind. I want every one of them miners droolin', like hungry dogs sittin' and watchin' a fresh-cooked Thanksgiving turkey bein' carved. I want 'em keen. Understand?'

Sarah didn't reply except for a curt nod.

'OK, and remember that ya need to smile a little, but not too much, we don't want a riot. If anybody asks questions, or talks money, you keep yer trap shut. That's business talk . . . leave all that kinda stuff to me.' He raised his hand and waved her towards the river. 'Move; get stripped and into that water before I toss you in, we ain't got all friggin' day.'

★ ★ ★

In the cool light of dawn, Sailor put the finishing touches to the travois he had rigged and strapped to one of his two mules.

'Right-oh mate, come on,' he said, turning to help Jimmy on to the canvas stretched and tied between the poles. 'Time for you and me to move along and maybe find a doctor for you.'

With his face twisting from stabs of pain, reluctantly the youth allowed himself to be gently manhandled on to the contraption.

'Don't forget my shotgun, will ya?'

'You're fussing like an old hen. No, I'll not forget your gun nor your saddle, lie back and enjoy the ride, everything's taken care of.'

While Sailor lashed his splinted limbs to the poles to keep him safe, Jimmy looked backward over his head to find himself staring up at the mule's backside.

'Hey, Sailor,' he confided, 'I sure

hope this animal of yours don't have the skitters.'

'Don't you worry none, son, even if she had you could be worse off.' The old prospector chuckled at the thought. 'If this was someplace like India or Burma that mule might be an elephant.'

On the third day of the tortuous journey, Jimmy developed a high fever. In spite of the care lavished upon him, he lapsed into unconsciousness and spent a couple of days hovering between life and death.

During this time he suffered night-mares in which he watched a young man have his face blown apart again and again. And there was a girl, a girl whom, although vaguely familiar, he could not recognize. She would drift in and out of his dreams, smile at him, then fade. That was always the time he would find himself falling down a bottomless pit and screaming.

Eventually the fever broke and he awoke bathed in sweat and having his

139

face wiped with a cool wet rag. A full moon was up and in the distance a lone coyote called to his far-off mate.

'Steady son, don't move them legs of yours or you'll wish you hadn't.'

Jimmy twisted his head and focused upon the smiling but relieved face of Sailor lit by the yellow light of a storm lantern.

'Glad to have you back, lad. For a time back there when you had the screamin' heebie-jeebies and I had t' hold ya down, I doubted you would live to see another sunrise.'

Jimmy frowned and gazed in awe into the old man's tired face.

'Mister?'

It was Sailor's turn to frown. The boy's voice was strangely hesitant . . . fearful even.

'What, lad?'

'Tell me, mister, who am I . . . what's my name?'

9

The mining camp stretched along both banks of the river. For more than a mile it nestled at the base of the vertical granite cliffs of the gorge which towered on either side. Marked clearly with the name of the hopeful owner, each claim had been meticulously staked out and roped or fenced off to prevent arguments and gun-fights. Some of the more flamboyant prospectors had fixed up boards already bearing the title of the prospector's dreams, such as The Million Dollar Strike, Sam's Fortune, or just something as simple as Mine!

Sarah noted the scattered rows of ragged canvas tents, a broken-wheeled Conestoga wagon, lean-to shacks and a few better built log cabins and even a large barrel laid on its side. It seemed to her that anything would act as a home in this place.

Men were everywhere, scurrying about like ants, building, hauling logs on chains behind horses to the saw-pits to turn them into lumber. Men stripped to the waist stood in the river erecting a log bridge to connect them with those on the other bank. All manner of things strange to her eyes intrigued and overwhelmed her. Every job the miners did appeared to call out hurry, hurry, hurry.

Sweating miners working half-clad or wearing filthy long-johns, pushed barrows of broken rock out from gaping holes at the base of the cliffs. They tipped their spoil into ingeniously constructed rocker boxes watered by sluice chutes which in turn emptied into multi-layered sieves where eagle-eyed men watched for and retrieved any gold dust. Other gold-seekers of less means or ingenuity were up to their knees in the shallows of the river, with feet wide apart they crouched and stared hopefully into their humble round-bottomed prospecting pans.

One by one the picks and hammers stopped swinging as the men became aware of the newcomers riding toward the centre of the camp. In a ripple of movement the miners straightened their backs to stand gazing open-mouthed directly at Nick and Sarah sharing the same horse.

'Smile,' Nick reminded her without turning round to check. Then a few seconds later asked, 'You smilin'?'

'Yes!' she answered through clenched teeth.

'Not too much, a little smile is all they get for free, we don't want t' spoil them.'

By this time men were dropping their tools and hurrying to catch up to and follow the newcomers. One of the miners yelled with glee.

'Jesus, it's Nick . . . he's done it. Yeah, good old Nick. See, he's gone and fetched us a new whore just like he said he would.'

'Yeah,' another responded with enthusiasm. 'Take an eyeful of her, she's young and a real good looker.'

'You said it, fella,' his partner drooled. 'Nobody I know would kick her out of the sack.'

Drawing ever closer the excited men pushed and shoved to get within touching distance of the girl. They began to shout directly at the male rider.

'Hey, Nick, I'll pay double if ya let me have the first night with her.'

'You ain't got enough in yer poke, Waldo,' Nick grinned back at the bidder.

'How much you charge, eh Nick?' another butted in, only to be ignored and denied even a derisive grin.

'Ya want t' make a straight trade for your woman?' another offered, pushing through the others to get close to the horse. 'I'll swap half my claim for sole rights in the little lady; it's lookin' real good and showin' plenty of yella already.'

'Forget it. There ain't one of ya who has enough money to buy this woman off me,' Nick yelled back suddenly, so loud that he could be heard above the others. Pulling up the horse he grinned and looked around at the eager faces pushing to take a closer look at Sarah. 'This here female,' he told them, thumbing in her direction, 'is Flossie. Flossie's my woman, and I'll rip the throat out of anybody who thinks she ain't.' He eyed all those around him. 'Savvy?'

An angry murmur of disappointment spread through the crowd as their hopes were dashed.

'It ain't right one man havin' her all to his self,' a voice barked out from the outside of the crowd. 'He's only one man against all of us. Snakes alive, we could take her now if we had a mind to.'

Then Sarah's blood chilled as she heard Nick's next reply.

'Who mentioned anythin' about anybody havin' her all to his lonesome?' Nick carried on smiling as he talked, but he slid the shotgun from its holster all the same and rested it across the saddle in front of him 'Hell, fellas, I sure didn't, I'm one of the sharing kind.'

A more hopeful murmur arose from the assembled men. They smiled happily again, many licked their lips, staring at Sarah as though in anticipation of a good meal. Others slicked down their hair and exchanged knowing glances with those nearby.

'Anyone of ya can have a taste of her . . . at a price, of course. But be warned, all of yers. This gal don't come cheap. No sir, she's kind of special and costs more than you're used t' payin' for ordinary whores. And there's gonna be no credit, so don't anyone ask. It's all pay on the nail or go without . . . understand?'

'Well, mister, I won't do it,' Sarah snarled in his ear and made a move to dismount. 'Not for you or anyone else in this God-forsaken place. I'd die first.'

His free hand gripped her above the

knee, his powerful fingers digging deep into the soft flesh like talons, hurting and preventing her from dismounting. Without losing the grin from his face he spoke in a low menacing voice.

'Killin' you'd be easy, but not good for profit,' he growled at her 'Now shut your stupid mouth or, just for the hell of it, I'll strip ya down to your bare hide here and now and sell ya to the highest bidder. And don't you think I won't.' Twisting his head around to look her in the face he scowled and suggested, 'Now do like I friggin'-well told ya in the first place, crack that frosty face of yours an' smile!'

Feeling her resistance ebb he released his grip on her thigh and she made no further attempt to disobey. Nudging the horse into a walk again he forced a passage through the jostling throng. Soon they were passing by the biggest tent Sarah had ever seen, outside and above the doorway of which a giant canvas banner proclaimed: 'GATEWAY TO HEAVEN, (WHISKEY AND WOMEN ALL

AT COMPETITIVE RATES).

Beneath this flapping banner, a trio of grossly overweight women sneered and cat-called Sarah whom they obviously perceived as serious competition to their trade. Dressed only in jaded knee-length drawers and grubby whalebone corsets from which bulging rolls of fat threatened to burst free with every movement made, they taunted and yelled like banshees.

'Just take a good gander at her,' the fattest of the three painted whores pointed, then wagged a podgy finger at Sarah and bawled to the drooling menfolk nearby. 'Look at her, fellas; see, there ain't a pickin' on her. She's thin as a straw,' she jeered. 'Any of you boys who lies with that skinny bitch is gonna have her bones stickin' between his own before he's halfway finished humpin' her once.'

'You're right, Frenchy,' a second whore broke in with her mock southern drawl. 'Why I do declare, she's got less meat on her than an undernourished rattlesnake.'

'Yeah,' the last of the trio shouted. 'That dame's so thin if she sneezed she'd whip a fella t' death.'

As she ended her tirade, a well-dressed man smoking a cigar and displaying several gold teeth as he grinned, came out from the tent and whipped her on the butt with his walking cane causing her to yelp.

'Shut up, Lulu, you give me earache,' he commanded. The fat prostitute rubbed at her ample backside to reduce the sting, but made no reply to either her boss's jibe or his punishment. Instead she stepped meekly aside on the duck-board, letting him pass to approach and speak to Nick. 'Nice merchandise you've got there, my friend,' he stated affably, nodding towards Sarah. 'Step down, come inside and have a drink. Maybe we can do business together?'

Nick did not bother to pull up. Instead he contemptuously spat a stream of tobacco juice and spittle in the brothel-keeper's direction, splashing his white frilled shirt to leave it stained with numerous dark-brown patches.

'Mister, don't talk shit,' Nick told him casually. 'You ain't ever been my friend, and as for you an' me doin' business . . . you can pucker up and kiss my ass.'

Miners laughed outright and the whores giggled, but the man with the gold teeth narrowed his eyes and glared his hatred. Before spinning on his heel and angrily pushing past his ponderous workers to go back into the confines of his tent, he whispered to himself.

'You won't spit at me or make a fool of me again, my friend . . . or for that matter, anyone else. I swear it.'

The tent had been partitioned off into a bar at one side and semi-private cubicles where each of the girls could do their work at the other. These cubicles were entered from a narrow passage which led from one end of the tent to the other. The furious brothel-keeper stormed into the last of these divisions which had the word PRIVATE painted directly on to the canvas door.

From the top drawer of a small battered desk he took out a sawn-off twelve-gauge shotgun professionally fitted with a pistol butt. Snapping the weapon open he loaded both barrels and stuffed a handful of extra cartridges into his coat pocket.

'Friend,' he sniggered, 'you're not going to make a dime of profit out of that girl. Not one dangblasted cent.' Cautiously lifting the rear wall of the tent he peeped out, checking that nobody was there to see him leave. Satisfied it was safe to do so, he scrambled out while holding the shotgun concealed in his jacket.

Keeping out of sight, he carefully made his way along the base of the cliff, furtively moving from cover to cover until he arrived beside a one-hole privy standing between the back of a cabin and the cliff. Cautiously he moved his head to peer round the corner of the privy wall. The cabin still had all of its shutters shut tight. Seeing his opportunity he slunk to the front of the privy. Its door swung open on rawhide hinges and gratefully he ducked into the safety of its stinking interior and leaned his back against the rough log wall in order to compose himself.

His breathing came in gasps and he could feel his heart thudding against his ribs. Carefully he took out the sawn-off and, with trembling fingers, drew back both hammers. Using one foot to wedge the privy door only wide enough to permit him to see the outside of the nearest window, he settled down to wait for the cabin's shutters to be opened wide.

'Come on, friend,' he whispered to himself. 'Forget the randy crowd. Come on, open up the shutters and let me see your face for only one more time.'

★ ★ ★

152

The torrential rains of the rare summer storm had washed away any trail there had been long before Mark Craythorn rode through the pass. Already familiar with the area, the lack of tracks did not bother him. Besides, knowing the mining camp Sarah and Jim Handly had been heading for, when he arrived at the Y junction of the pass, he unhesitatingly turned on to the correct trail.

'Well, boy,' he said to his horse as they descended the slope, 'that's one good thing we can be sure of; if the storm's washed the kids' tracks away for me, then the Baxter clan ain't going to have any help with 'em neither.'

Joining the forest trail, the sheriff discovered that the conditions were vastly different to what they had been on the previous occasions he had passed that way. The warming rays of the sun had been prevented by the shielding overhead branches from drying the ground, the result of this being that the tremendous downpour had turned the forest floor into a vast bog of mud and sodden dead leaves.

Unused to such horrendous conditions, the sheriff's horse constantly sank up to its hocks in the cloying mire. Each and every step took a supreme effort and within minutes the struggling animal was blowing hard as if he had been galloping for an hour or more.

With such an unequal battle to move forward at all, it quickly became clear to the lawman that getting through to the diggings was going to take much longer than had been planned. Craythorn decided it would be easier if he took his weight off his horse.

'All right, fella,' he sighed resignedly as he dismounted. 'I get the message, but don't you plan on making this a habit.' Taking the reins in his right hand he took the lead. His reluctant mount followed walking and pulling his hooves clear of the goo with the same loud sucking noises as before but using far less effort.

In such adverse conditions the journey

through the forest was bound to be long and tedious.

* * *

When the Baxters rode into town, Bart asked the first person they laid eyes on where the diggings were. The old-timer stared at them as if they were loco. Then he grinned broadly.

'Well, they sure ain't anywhere near here.' His wizened hand pointed back the way they had travelled. 'You notice a fork in the road way back as you came down from the pass . . . kind of narrow and steep like it don't want to go nowhere in a hurry?'

'Ah hell!' Luke cursed. 'Pa, didn't I say that was the trail we should've taken, didn't I, eh? As soon as we reached it I . . . '

'Boy, unless you want a punch in the jaw,' Bart Baxter advised, 'shut up!' He turned to the oldtimer again who had already hobbled on his way, and called out. 'Is there a saloon with a bar in this one-horse town?'

'Sure. One on either side of Main Street,' he called back laconically over his shoulder. 'Even you fellas should be able to find one of 'em.'

'Smart-assed old goat,' Bart grumbled. Saddleweary and feeling old, he looked forward to leaning on a bar with a bottle of red-eye, and the sound of a piano in the background. Maybe a dancing girl to soothe him, to whisper in his ear, telling him things he had not heard for a long time. Maybe private, suggestive things. He didn't care what she looked like . . . at his age all of them looked good. Inspired by his momentary daydream he abruptly informed the others, 'We stay here for the night.'

The morning was already as hot as a blacksmith's forge when the Baxters, dull-eyed and each one nursing a hangover, reluctantly mounted up and rode out of town back the way they had come. After a hectic night in soft beds with hard-working women they were weary. Their limbs ached and each man secretly wished he did not have to ride on that particular day.

Halfway to the fork in the trail, Matt caught their attention by calling out and pointing into the distance.

'Hey, there's a guy out there, he's waving at us. His mule, its haulin' a travois. Maybe someone's sick or hurt?'

'Yeah, maybe down with the small-pox. Let him wave. We've got troubles of our own . . . them Handlys for instance,' Bart reminded them. 'We ain't got time to pass the time o' day with the likes of him.' Spurring his horse he urged them, 'Come on, boys, get the lead out.'

★ ★ ★

Sailor watched with a mixture of anger and dismay as the mounted men ignored his signals to stop.

'The lousy bastards, they ain't human,' he exploded and dashed his already battered hat to the ground in disgust as the horsemen put on speed and rode on. 'Well, I hope you'll need help one day, mates,' he yelled after them even though the distance was too great for them to hear. 'And I hope your balls rot and fall off before you get it.'

Stopping the mule he unhooked his canteen from the panniers, shook it, and pursed his lips at the hollow sound it made.

'Damned near empty.'

Jim's fever had returned and once again he lay delirious and oblivious of the world around him. Sailor uncorked the canteen and eased a few drops of the precious water in between the youth's parched lips.

'Hold on, mate, there's a town I know near here, I'll get you to a sawbones if it kills me.'

★ ★ ★

'This place,' Nick said to the gold seekers, as he thumbed over his shoulder at the cabin, 'opens at eight tonight. I advise ya all to go and weigh out your dust ready to bid if ya want to be first to have a nibble at the cherry.'

'She still got her cherry?' a surprised miner asked in awe.

'Every time,' Nick winked, and gave a lecherous grin. 'Now leave us be. The lady has to rest and get herself ready for you randy bulls.' Acting ten feet tall, the centre of attention and with the prospect of soon being worth more than he had ever been, he clearly enjoyed every moment.

Dismounting outside his cabin, he waved the shotgun high above his head.

'See ya tonight, boys.' With that he hitched the horse and mules to the rail in front of the cabin, nodded for Sarah to get down while he loosed off the lashings on the panniers.

'Go on inside, Flossie, light the stove, make me some coffee and make a start t' tidy the place ready. I'll see to the horse an' the unloadin' of the pack mules.'

The heavy split-log door sagged on its top hinge and she had to use all her weight to noisily scrape the bottom edge through the dried mud covering on the floor. The wedge of sunlight widened, illuminating the single room to reveal food-caked tin plates piled in a filthy bucket on a table covered with dust and grime. Flies hummed everywhere and the dust-laden webs of spiders were to be seen in every nook and cranny. Dirty long-johns and other equally grubby clothing had been liberally scattered all around.

Sarah wrinkled her nose in disgust.

'This place stinks like a hog's backside,' she announced to no one in particular. 'Let's have some air before I choke.'

One by one she removed the stout wooden bars holding the shutters secure and opened them as wide as they would go. However, as luck would have it, one shutter gave her trouble. Situated on the rear wall, the bar had dried out, twisted and bowed so much that she found that she could not budge it.

While she struggled to release this particular bar, Nick entered carrying the shotgun and some supplies from the panniers. He scowled.

'You still pissin' about? Ya goin' t' take all friggin' day t' do that?'

'I can't help it, this bar's held too tight,' she argued.

In disgust, he deposited the gun and supplies on one end of the table before stomping across to where she struggled.

'Get out of the friggin' way,' he sniggered pushing her aside. 'Hit the dangled thing, don't tickle it.' With one fist he thumped the heavy bar up and free and pushed the shutters open wide.

As soon as the light flooded in the most recently opened window, there was a terrifically loud bang from outside. In utter surprise, Sarah watched a spray of red appear to burst and float around the head of the man who had raped her. Blasted backwards he crashed on to the floor to lay spreadeagled and motionless. Nick existed no longer, he was dead and had completely lost his face.

The instinct for self-preservation warned her to snatch the gun from the table and, as she did so, she became aware of a different noise coming from outside the same window. Clicking back the hammers she swung round in time to see Nick's killer standing with his head and shoulders framed in the opening as he peered inside.

His staring eyes swiftly searched the gloom inside the cabin until they fixed upon her. His lips drew back to show his teeth and his eyes narrowed when he brought up his sawn-off to bring it to bear on herself.

She did not wait for him to fire. With her own gun already roughly in line with the whorehouse-owner's upper chest, but still only held waist-high to herself, she squeezed both triggers.

With the simultaneous discharge of both barrels the recoil of her twelve-gauge almost tore the weapon free of her grasp, but she held on. Her spontaneous aim had been a little high and the concentrated load of lead buckshot caught her target in his throat, a mite lower down than his Adam's apple.

One moment he had been standing there ready to kill her, then his head disappeared. A fountain of bright red blood from a severed artery immediately squirted skywards before the body slowly sagged and dropped from view. Only the blood dropping from above the window showed he had once been there at all.

Although she had never planned to do so, she had killed another man. Stunned by this undreamed of turn of events she looked at the smoking gun held in her hands, then at the corpse on the floor. The gory scene sickened her and she turned away from the gruesome sight.

As the distant sound of shouting came to her ears, her eyes came to rest on a duffel-bag among the things Nick had brought in. The bag belonged to her, it held the rest of her clothes. More men were shouting and when she glanced out from one of the side windows she could see excited miners racing towards the cabin.

What should she do? If she stayed there she could be accused of murder. She could be lynched . . . or worse.

In a trice she had made up her mind. Grabbing the duffel-bag she hitched up the skirt of her dress and ran outside. Shoving the shotgun into its saddle holster she hung the bag on the horn of the saddle and freed the reins from the rail. Then almost as the first men arrived at the cabin she swung up into the saddle and rode off, hell for leather.

With the river flowing on her left and the cliff towering on her right, there was only one route she could take, that which led her upstream, away from the yelling fist-shaking men.

10

When Mark Craythorn finally left the deep shade and cloying mud of the forest behind he felt better. Making for the river, he bathed himself and groomed his horse to get rid of the caked-on mud, then together they rested, basking in the sunshine until they were dry.

'Have any of you men seen a lanky kid and his sister ride into camp lately?' Craythorn asked the first group of men he ran into in the mining camp.

'Nope,' answered a lean, grey-bearded prospector cutting a wad of tobacco. 'There ain't been any kids since them two brothers came here last year. Greenhorns. They both died, got buried by a roof-fall, diggin' into the bottom of the cliff, remember them don't ya, Zach?'

'I ain't interested in somebody from

that far back,' Craythorn stated. 'The kids I'm talking about were real keen to prospect for gold. They should have arrived here in the last few days. They both had horses and led a couple of mules with plenty of provisions. Oh, yes, and they each had shotguns. A nice couple of kids. The boy was kind of proud of his gun . . . always cleaning it and showing it off to folks.' He stopped talking when they all stood shaking their heads.

The one called Zach piped up suddenly as though emerging from a trance.

'The only two folks who rode in this week were a one-eyed guy who came back here after leavin' for a few days. Went by the name of Nick. Brought a young female with him, a good-lookin' gal but she was just a whore same as the other three here. Didn't seem to like him much neither, and yet they both shared the saddle of the same horse. Come to think on it, Nick had a pair of mules in tow I ain't ever seen before, and they were sure carrying plenty of vittles an' supplies.'

'That's right,' one of the others chipped in. 'There was all kinds of prospectin' tools an' things. and all brand new by the looks of 'em.' He poked his nose thoughtfully. 'Never could understand that. I mean, what kind of guy spends good money on tools an' stuff if he intends to sit back and let a whore do the moneymaking', it don't make sense, do it?'

'And that one-eyed Nick fella,' another blurted out. 'He didn't leave here with as much as a lead nickel, I know that for a certain fact. He lost his whole poke and everything but his cabin to the big Swede. All in a single hand of poker.'

'Yeah, that's right. I was there when he lost out. Thought he was going to knife the Swede, but he didn't. Then he lit out on the mornin' of the very next day . . . and he was on foot. With no horse, no nothin'.'

'When he came back with the woman,'

poker-faced, Craythorn concealed his growing interest, 'which direction did they come from?'

'Same way as you, from the pass and through the trees. Got here the day after the night of the storm.'

'I'd like to have a talk with them,' Craythorn explained. 'Maybe they can help me?'

'Doubt it,' the lean prospector broke into a grin.

'I'll be the judge of that. Where are they?'

'One of them shot the other dead and then high-tailed it out of here.'

'Murder?'

'Well, they weren't playin' pat-a-cake, fella.'

'Who did the shooting?'

'The woman, there ain't no doubt about that. Funny though, she looked as sweet as blueberry pie. But she still pulped his face at point-blank range with a shotgun.'

Zach joined in again.

'Guess she didn't like him much

168

because when she skedaddled, the guy who owned the whores around here, he went along with her.' He spat and rubbed the spittle into the dust with his toe. 'Never could understand that. Imagine a guy leavin' with one whore and leavin' three more behind, along with everything else he owned?'

The lawman frowned and stroked his chin.

'They take the mules with them?'

'Nope . . . only the horse.

'Just one horse? Didn't the whore-house man have a horse?'

The prospectors gaped at each other.

'Now why didn't any of us think of that? That animal's still hitched by the big tent. I know, because I saw big fat Ella feedin' it this mornin'.'

Knowing that the Handly kids would never have separated from each other voluntarily, the sheriff now feared the worst. By simple deduction he reasoned that if the girl who had carried out the murder was Sarah, then her kid brother was probably dead.

'You or anyone else see them go?'

'Sure, a few of us did. We ran down there after we heard a couple of shots.' Pausing for a moment he scratched at his nose. 'Come to think back on it, I do believe I'm tellin' you an untruth, mister.' He scratched at his nose again. 'Now, that's right, it was just the woman. I can't rightly recollect seeing the brothel-keeper.'

'How about the rest of you, is that the same as you all saw?'

'We saw the girl all right, she galloped off like the Devil himself was after her along with all the demons in Hell.'

'And the brothel-keeper . . . did anybody see him leave with her?'

'No, but he sure didn't hang around. Everybody saw him go into the big tent a short while before the shootin'. He ain't been seen since. It's clear to me he must've known that new girl from somewhere else and maybe had some sort of plan made with her.'

'Couldn't have,' Zach argued. 'Didn't have time t' arrange anything, did he?

Think on it, he's been tradin' here for months.'

'Well, he ain't been seen since the dang-blasted shootin' has he? But I'll tell ya this much: if he don't come back his girls won't mind none. They're makin' a whole barrel of money.' Chuckling, he added, 'I'll bet none of them fat whores have had their knee-bones touched together for more than five minutes since he left.'

'Where are the mules and the supplies now?'

The lean one squinted thoughtfully at Craythorn.

'Ya know, fella, for a stranger who we don't know from shit, you sure want answers to a lot of questions.'

'Hey, that's right,' Zach agreed. 'Who the hell are you, mister . . . what's yer business?'

With his jaw square set, Craythorn eyed them one by one after he pulled his jacket aside and displayed his tin star.

'Craythorn's the name and my

business is the law.'

Avoiding his eyes, to a man they looked down at their feet and shuffled them in the dust, acting as guilty as schoolboys caught stealing apples from a neighbour's orchard.

'You men got a miners' council in this camp?'

'Uh-huh . . . sort of.'

'I want to talk to the elected chairman. And I don't want any horsing around; I mean, I want to see him now!'

★ ★ ★

'Think the lad'll live, Doc?' Sailor asked with concern in his voice when the doctor came out to speak with him on the porch.

The medical man pursed his lips and rocked his open hand to indicate the situation to be touch and go.

'Taking an educated guess, if he survives through the next couple of days and if we beat the fever, he's got a fifty-fifty chance.'

'Then it could still go either way?'

'That's the cold down-to-earth statistics of it. But don't worry, the young man has a great deal going for him. My wife's a fine nurse; I should know, we worked together all through the war. She never gave up on a patient and often pulled them clear of the grim reaper's scythe.'

'And will he be able to walk and move around under his own sail?'

'Don't see why not. You did as good a job of his broken bones as most trained doctors.'

Sailor nodded.

'It isn't the first time I've done that job.' Then he abruptly changed the subject. 'Tell me what it costs and I'll settle up with you any time you like. I have a bit put aside for hard times, so don't stint with the boy.'

The doctor laughed and slapped Sailor heartily on the back as he escorted him towards the gate and the waiting mule.

'Stint? My wife will spoil that boy something rotten . . . as if he's our own son. We've never had any family of our own, and it's hit her hard, so she tends to over-compensate whenever she gets the chance.'

'Opportunities lost, eh? Well, I know the feelin', Doc. Believe me, I know it well.'

* * *

Beneath the closed green canopy of the forest, the conditions under foot were still wet and swampy. The air was as humid as it was possible to be without actually raining.

'Jesus but this is tough,' Matt Baxter gasped as he helped to haul a horse out of the mud for the third time that day. 'I sure hope all this sweatin's been worth the effort I've put in to it.'

'What d'ya mean? 'You've put in'. You ain't done no different to the rest

174

of us,' Luke growled. 'I bet you ain't even blistered yer hands.'

'Quit that squabbling and get on with it,' Bart ordered. 'Sometimes I think I'd be better off if yer momma had presented me with daughters, instead of bellyaching, layabout mavericks.'

'I ain't bellyachin', Pa,' Dale exclaimed.

'I know that, son. I guess I was just mouthin' off at the others.'

'One of these days the old man'll be buyin' Dale one of them coats of many colours, like that guy in the Bible,' Luke sniggered to Matt.

'What you sayin', boy?' his father called out. 'You smart-mouthin' about me . . . are yer, eh?'

'Me, Pa?' Luke asked, his face the picture of innocence. 'I wouldn't do that. Not t' you, Pa.'

The edges of Bart's tight-lipped mouth turned downwards as he glared at the offender, uncertain. After a tense moment he scowled and uttered a warning.

'Then see ya don't . . . unless you're

lookin' to get the whippin' of yer life.'

* * *

Once Sarah was confident that no posse of lynch-happy miners pursued her, she slowed down and rode into the rocky shallows of the river. Staying there for about the next three miles helped to hide her tracks and let her horse cool off. Finally she selected an easy rocky slope on the opposite bank, guided her mount from the water and dismounted.

Taking stock of her immediate future while her horse happily snuffled and dragged mouthfuls of grass, her spirits dived to the depths of despair. Her future did not look good. No food, no money to buy any with, only a horse, her father's old shotgun and a bagful of her clothes.

Remembering the saddle-bags, she reached up behind the saddle and eagerly felt under the covering flaps of each hoping that Nick had not changed the contents.

'A box of cartridges for the twelve-gauge, about twenty, that's good. Bag of coffee, billy-can, a knife, tin mug and small sack of . . . ' Eagerly undoing the cord which fastened the neck she plunged in a hand. Her spirits sagged once again. 'Beans, beans, beans. Plenty of lousy beans.' Disgusted she returned the beans to the sack and tied the neck again.

'God in Heaven.' Dramatically she raised her hands and eyes skywards. 'Beans! Lord, it just ain't fair. Ya know how I've always hated the darn things, they make me fart worse than my horse.'

11

'This is the place in here, Sheriff, this is where the shootin' was done.' The head man of the miners' council opened the door of the cabin and ushered Craythorn inside. 'There.' He pointed the toe of his boot and numerous flies buzzed up from a patch of blood which had dried and blackened on the floor. 'Nick, the guy who got himself killed here, never did look good, but take my word for it, that shotgun didn't improve him one bit.'

After inspecting the area immediately around the bloodstain, the sheriff widened his search and wandered round the unkempt room.

'Where's all the vittles and stuff they brought here?' he asked suddenly. 'Everything they had loaded on the two mules?'

The other man flushed and looked

away as he stammered a reply.

'Stuff . . . Sheriff? Don't know anything about anything. That's gospel or may the Lord strike me dead.'

Craythorn caught hold of the man's jacket and pulled him until he came close to kissing distance.

'Well, mister, you're the one who got himself elected top man around here, so it's up to you to find out, and I mean within the hour.'

The top man's eyes bulged, his mouth hung open and he swallowed audibly as Craythorn carried on with his demands.

'I want them mules and every last thing they were carrying. I don't care if it's only a nail or something as big as a pot-bellied stove, I want all of it brought here. If I have to start searching through this camp myself, believe me, there'll be arrests made.'

'I can't do that,' the man objected.

'You better. Unless that is, you aim to become prime suspect in the murder. Murder's a hanging offence, even for

179

those who aid the killer.'

'Murder . . . me? That's all hogwash, you know I didn't have anythin' to do with the shootin'.'

Craythorn smiled pleasantly. 'You know that . . . I know that but you try and convince a jury of that. Juries usually play safe and stand by the officers of the law.' He tapped his badge with a finger, then smiled again. 'Did you hear that? An officer of the law . . . that's me.' Pushing the crimson-faced man away from him he pointed to the door. 'One hour,' he reminded.

'You bastard!' the miner snapped, then he stomped out.

The buzzing of flies drew Craythorn's attention to an open window in the rear wall. Automatically he glanced outside. Between the cabin and the cliff, a privy stood with its door wide open. His attention was drawn to what he took to be a ball on the ground, midway between the privy and the cabin. But, this ball was different: this one was smothered in flies.

'Jesus,' he breathed as the truth dawned. 'That's somebody's head.' He looked down. Below him, the nattily dressed late owner of the head lay crumpled.

Close by the open left hand of the torso lay a sawn-off shotgun. At a glance he noted that one of its hammers had remained cocked. The weapon's shortened barrels no longer gave off that familiar cared-for gleam of a firearm, for already they were rusting.

Clambering out through the window and jumping down beside the cadaver, Craythorn first of all checked the contents of the pockets. An abundance of money, a silk handkerchief, an emerald ring, together with a gold watch and chain, all told him the motive had *not* been robbery. The head had not been decapitated by the blade of a sharp implement such as an axe or a sword, for the flesh was not smoothly cut. Instead the edges of the neck-wound were ragged and torn as if the head had been dragged from it by enormous hands.

Upon examination of the privy door he discovered spatters of blood and holes made by lead pellets. He dug out a couple of these with his knife.

'Hmm,' he said, pursing his lips thoughtfully. 'Hmm.' Crossing to pickup and check the sawn-off he let down the cocked hammer and removed the unfired cartridge. 'Huh! Bird-shot. This guy was no gambler; he sure didn't risk missing at close range.'

★ ★ ★

A constant stream of surly grumbling miners returned the mules and most of what the animals had been carrying when last the sheriff had seen them in the possession of the Handlys.

'Satisfied?' the sweating and panting chairman of the miners' committee asked, when the last of the missing goods were assembled on the ground.

'Now maybe you'll stop hassling us and get after that murderin' harlot.'

'Yeah,' someone called. 'Get the bitch strung up.'

'And that son-of-a-bitch whore-master who went along with her.'

Sheriff Craythorn stood waiting quietly until the commotion died down. Only when there was silence did he commence to speak to them.

'First of all there isn't going to be any hanging. Not for this particular crime.' A commotion erupted but he fired two shots into the air and caught everyone's attention again.

'That ain't right, Sheriff,' argued the top man again, eager to regain his standing with the others. 'You said yourself there's been a crime committed. She ought to hang. She's got to.'

Craythorn's head shook slowly from side to side.

'The first thing you men should know, is that there were two killings . . . but only one murder.' As slick as a stage magician he produced the gold watch he had removed from the dead man and held it up for all to see. A murmur rippled round the spectators. 'Ah, I can see you recognize it.'

'Of course we do. We all do. Anybody who humped his whores can tell ya who that belongs to. He used to time us by it when we were in with one of the gals.'

'Well, he won't use it to time you any more,' Craythorn announced to happy and tumultuous applause, then he waved them back down to silence again. 'That particular gentleman won't time you ever again.'

'We all knew that when he skedaddled with the new gal, didn't we, fellas?'

'And that's where you're wrong again.' The sheriff raised his voice. 'That's where you're *all* wrong.' Silence blanketed the crowd once more.

'And you know why?' He waited, letting their curiosity build. 'No? I thought not. Well, I'll tell you. Because the last owner of this watch . . . he's had his head blown off his shoulders.'

'Oh yeah, who said?' the same man asked again.

'Me!' the sheriff thumbed his chest angrily. 'I do. If any of you had taken the time to look around the back of this here cabin, instead of pilfering whatever you could lay your greedy hands on, you would have found him and his head.'

'Yippee!' The happy scream came from one of the prostitutes who had joined the crowd. 'Then he sure isn't comin' back. We ain't got a boss no more.'

'Shut yer fool mouth, woman,' yelled the elected leader. 'Anyhow, what ya doin' here? This business is serious. It's *men's* business.'

'And you think I ain't?' she laughed. 'Hell, fella, I ain't ever been so serious in my whole darned life. As for *men's business*. I'll tell ya all right here and now, me and my partners are surely lookin' forward to lots of that.'

'Sheriff, now that gal's got to be

caught and hanged, even you've got to agree with that. By any reckoning, killin' two men is enough to hang even a saint.'

'Some folk never listen. She didn't shoot two men . . . only one.' Craythorn held up the watch for all to see again. She blew the head off the man who owned this. But it wasn't murder, it was good old self-defence, and no one hangs for that.'

'How about Nick, she shot him, didn't she?'

'No, the other guy did that, and then he was killed as he was about to fire at the girl.'

'Jesus, I don't believe all this talk. Mister, have you been on the moonshine or somethin'? You weren't even there, but you stand there tellin' us things as if you'd seen 'em with yer own eyes. That whore's guilty as sin and we all know it.' He turned to the rest of the men. 'We know that, don't we, fellas?'

A babble of agreement went up

from the angry miners. But Craythorn merely discharged another shot into the air from his pistol and, as before, the noise settled.

'Give your jaws a rest and listen, then maybe you'll understand how things happened inside that cabin the other day. Nick and the girl were inside. He must've opened the last of the window shutters in the back wall. That's a pretty safe bet because those are the only shutters which ain't held back to the wall. Why? Because he didn't have time to do it. He didn't have the time, because the fella with the fancy watch was outside, waiting with both hammers of a sawn-off shotgun on full cock. When the gun discharged a barrel at point-blank range, Nick didn't stand a chance in hell. That single shot mashed his face and killed him instantly.'

The sea of faces before him were agog and quietly attentive, like children being told a bedtime story, so he continued, 'At that time of day the sun must have been well up, and reflecting off the cliff it would be bright enough to dazzle a blind man out there behind the cabin. To the killer, already close to the outside of the window, the inside of the cabin must have seemed dark and gloomy as he peered inside looking for the new girl. He didn't want to leave any witnesses, but the poor light inside the room would have been his downfall. While he waited the couple of seconds needed to adjust his eyes to see in those conditions, the frightened female must have grabbed Nick's gun. I reckon she fired only a gnat's whisker before he could line up and pull the trigger for the second barrel.'

He felt in his vest pocket, then held up a piece of distorted lead-shot between his finger and thumb.

'I picked this and another like it out of the door of the privy that's built directly in line with the window. For you guys at the back and can't see, it's buckshot. Terrified as she must've been, acting in a blind panic to save her own life, the girl probably jerked both triggers at the same time.' Shrugging his shoulders as if to state the obvious he added, 'When she fired, the slugs caught him full in the throat. Two loads of buckshot hitting there at that range would've blasted anyone's head off.'

'Then why wasn't Nick's head blowed off? He was gunned down from just about the same range, wasn't he, Sheriff?'

'That's true,' Craythorn agreed. 'But the other guy, he was only peppered with bird-shot and in the head. That stuff made a mess of his face and killed him, but that's about all it would do.'

'Ain't that enough?' The questioner burst into a grin and the crowd laughed, breaking the tension.

12

Afraid that even a small cooking fire would give her position away to a following posse, Sarah ate nothing hot on the first day after the shootings. However, during the days which followed, having seen no sign of any pursuit, she cast caution aside and used her gun to good effect shooting jack-rabbits for the pot.

Riding steadily, she followed the base of the mountain knowing such a route was bound to lead her to somewhere that had been civilized. One evening soon after sunset, she decided to make camp among some willows which would give her good cover from any searchers. Tired, with her limbs stiff and aching after a long day in the saddle, she made do with the almost inevitable cold rabbit meat she had saved from the day before.

The evening was still warm and she sat resting with her back to a tree as darkness descended. Suddenly, out of the corner of her eye a distant light blinked on, then another and another. Soon a whole lot of them flickered through the branches of the trees.

A posse, that was her first thought. Fear sent the hair crawling up the back of her neck. Could be randy fire-bugs, she reasoned and wanted to believe, until she realized that the lights were not moving. They could not be fire-bugs. But, she decided, on the other hand they were in the wrong direction to belong to a posse chasing after her.

Curious, but still as cautious as ever, Sarah took up her twelve-gauge and clicked back the hammers. Among the trees the night had grown much darker. She had to feel her way through straggling willows and bushes with sword-like thorns which drew blood from her hide on more than one occasion.

Where the trees thinned out they gave way to a mixture of bushes and tall coarse grass as high as bullrushes. Slowly she stood up and on tip-toe peered out over the thorny tops. From this position more lights were visible, all much further away than she had first imagined, and there were lots more of them. Some strung close together in rows, others scattered and further apart. She heaved a sigh and beamed a smile.

'Well, would ya believe it? Lamp-lit windows . . . it's a town,' she breathed in deeply, overawed and on the point of weeping. It was difficult to comprehend living in a proper place again, with real decent people, folks she could talk to and laugh with. Human beings who ate at tables, washed themselves and didn't stink like hogs.

Happy in her newly gained knowledge, Sarah gently eased back the hammers of the shotgun, turned and headed back to her camp. Off guard for only a moment, a thorn raked her cheek, reminding her that she was still alone with all the dangers in the wilderness.

'Damn it,' she cursed. 'Once I get myself out of this miserable God-forsaken hole, all the mules in the county wouldn't ever come near to haulin' me back. Not for man, land or gold. There ain't nothin, but nothin', that's worth the daily chore of stayin' alive out here.'

★ ★ ★

When they reached the edge of the mining camp the first prospector Bart Baxter questioned was up to his knees in water. Adeptly he kept on tilting the pan this way and that, working water over the gravel in his pan. Head down he spat into the river as though he didn't give a hoot about them or anyone else, then shook his head.

'Nope.' Raucously he cleared his throat and spat again. 'Ain't laid eyes on the pair yer seeking.'

'Aw, Pa,' Matt said. 'We know

they're here. They gotta be. This fella don't know shit from snow. Either that or he's lyin' through his teeth.'

'Matt's right, Pa, we knowed they were comin' here.' Luke backed up his brother. 'We knowed them Handlys bought mules an' every damn thing they needed to work a claim here. They've got to be hidin' away round here someplace.'

At this point all eyes were on Bart, waiting to hear his answer. That was why no one noticed the prospector tip out the gravel from his pan, rinse it, then hurl it spinning at Matt's head. His aim was accurate. The worn edge of the rotating pan struck horizontally and sliced through Matt's right ear, knocking him sideways from the saddle before it clanged down on to the riverbank shortly after he did.

'I don't ever allow anyone to call me a liar,' the prospector explained to them. 'That's on account that I ain't.'

Astounded by the sudden dramatic

tumble Matt had taken, the rest of the Baxters turned shocked eyes from the unconscious body, back to the old-timer standing tall and feet astride in the river. In his hand instead of his pan he now held a cavalry Colt which from their vulnerable position looked as big as a cannon and equally dangerous.

'Reach 'em high . . . all of ya.'

'Now, mister, there ain't no need to take this so dang seriously,' Bart smiled and was about to say more.

'Hands up!' The Colt's firing mechanism clicked ominously.

This time they all obeyed and, using his best diplomatic voice the father of the family kept the grin glued rigidly on his face.

'The boy meant nothing. Yer know how kids are these days. They always like to show off and score points over their elders.'

'If he'd been a kid I wouldn't have downed him that way,' the man pointing the gun explained. 'But he's a grown man and well due for a grown man's treatment.'

Matt groaned, the right side of his face and neck was bathed in blood which flowed freely on to his shirt and vest as he sat upright. Staggering to his feet he gladly grasped and held on to the stirrup of his saddle for support.

'What happened?' he asked, feeling at his bisected ear then looking stupidly at the blood on his hand afterwards.

'Ya shot yer fool mouth off once too often,' Bart growled.

Light dawned on Matt as his senses cleared. 'That dang-blasted prospector . . . I'll kill him.'

'I wouldn't try it, son,' Bart cautioned. 'Not unless you want a bullet-hole through yer thick skull as well as havin' a split ear.'

Without lowering his guard, the prospector placed two fingers of his free hand to his mouth then gave a series of loud whistles. In hardly any time at all the Baxters found themselves surrounded by men wielding shovels and pick-axes, all clearly more than ready for a fight. One of the newcomers broke into laughter and pointed at Matt's divided ear.

'Hey, boys, here's another smart-ass who's wearin' old Josh's personal brand.'

A tidal wave of laughter swept through the throng. One kicked Matt in the pants with such force that if the cowboy hadn't clung on to the stirrup he would have fallen on his face in the dust.

'Boys . . . fellas, please,' Bart Baxter pleaded to the miners. 'Be reasonable. We didn't come here to make any trouble. This whole thing's nothin' but a simple misunderstanding. It's a stupid mistake by my mule-headed boy. Ya can see he's already paid for that, so let's all be friendly, eh?'

'Friendly?' one with a pick-axe held at the ready asked with scorn. 'By your way of measuring things, how friendly is friendly?'

Bart paused to think of the meaning of the man's question.

'Well,' he said, 'I mean real friendly, like maybe there's someplace nearby where I can buy us all a drink.' He smiled. 'Aw, come on, fellas, no real harm's been done. What d'ya say?'

The miners exchanged meaningful glances with the prospector who had been wronged. He took his time, letting the Baxters sweat a little while considering Bart's offer, but nodded in agreement at long last. Everyone cheered as he holstered his weapon and waded out of the river and approached the Baxters. He addressed Bart.

'Mister, if I had a son who's foolish enough to get himself a gash in his lug such as he has, I'd wamp him real good, every morning before breakfast. That young fella, he needs to learn manners.' It was his turn to break into a grin. 'But as to your kind and mighty generous offer of buying us drinks,' he beamed up at the rancher, 'I don't know about the rest of you, but I always prefer to start a serious drinking session with a full bottle of red-eye . . . All to myself.'

★ ★ ★

Further upstream, Sheriff Craythorn took his time as he followed the river. Several times at regular intervals he left the loaded mules and crossed over to search the other bank before he found Sarah's trail.

'Smart-minded female,' he remarked to his horse. 'She's under more pressure than a woman should have, but still she's thinking ahead just the same as a man. You know, I've got to admit it, I always did respect signs of a logical mind in a woman. What do you say?'

The horse flicked an ear but as usual did not say a word. Craythorn grinned to himself.

'OK, be like that. I only hope she's brainy enough not to blow my head off if she sees me before I see her.'

A continuous squeaking and creaking of a bed on the other side of the canvas partition, coupled with a chorus of heavy snoring awoke Bart Baxter. Squeezing the sides of his head between the knuckles of his fists he attempted to fight against the brain-battering pain of his hangover.

Carousing with the miners and prospectors on the previous day had ended in the brothel tent and had cost him more cash than he liked to spend. Now, clad in only his sweat-soaked long-johns, he wished he was dead. His tongue felt as if a stable-boy had used it as a doormat, and neither of his eyes wanted to focus clearly on anything.

Turning on to his back caused his immediate world to wobble then spin around and he felt nauseous . . . doubly so when he discovered he was lying in bed next to a snoring woman. And what a woman! Naked as a fried egg, she had enough spare meat on her frame to feed a pack of starving wolves for a month.

With a compulsive choking cough she stirred. Her snoring stopped. Then she belched before, bleary-eyed, she turned her flabby face to his. Several of her concertina chins followed in quick succession and her pendulous breasts flopped over his arm, slapping down like sacks of tripe.

'Why, honey,' she simpered seductively, pressing her plentiful reserves of wobbling fat closer still. 'Ya sure are an early riser.' Lifting a cynical eyebrow she added, 'Still, I suppose a defenceless little gal like me just has to submit my body anytime a *big* man like you has the urge.'

Hauling his trapped arm from under her bust, Bart did his best to clamber out of bed, but she caught hold of his long-johns and held on as he retorted, 'Kiss my ass.'

'All right, honey, but that'll be a dollar extra. You have to pay a gal more for exotic work.'

With his bare feet on the dried mud on the duckboard floor, he pulled free of her. The ripping of cloth came loud and clear, and at the same moment he felt a draught of cold air where the back-flap of his long-johns had been.

'Jesus Christ, woman, did ya *have* to do that? This is the only pair I brought with me.'

The rhythmic squeaking of a bed on the other side of the partition grew to a rapid crescendo, then ceased. A panting voice called out, 'That you, Pa? Have ya got a chew of tobacco to spare?'

'Matt? No I ain't, so haul yourself up off that female yer tryin' to rock to sleep and go round-up yer brothers. You tell 'em an' tell 'em good, I want 'em all bright-eyed and bushy-tailed, mounted and ready to ride out in twenty minutes. I've got me a hangin' on my mind.'

'Ah, Pa!'

A female giggled, and the bed squeaked some more.

'Pronto, ya randy young buck,' Bart yelled, again clutching his head to subdue a fresh surge of pain. 'Get up off her. I mean now . . . not sometime when ya feel like it.'

13

The owner of the town livery stable paused work by the steaming mound of straw mixed with fresh horse manure. Resting one booted foot on the half-empty wheelbarrow he leaned on the handle of his pitchfork. As a polite gesture he twitched the brim before shoving his hat back from his sweating forehead. He nodded at the mare.

'You want stabling for her, miss?'

Sarah nodded, gave a brief hesitant smile which barely showed her teeth.

'Yeah, I want stabling, all right, but as well as that I'm lookin' out for a job.' Before he could interject she went on quickly, 'I'm real good with horses, mister. My folks used to own a small herd bred mainly for ridin'. Had 'em since I was just a kid.' Affectionately she patted her mount's shoulder. 'This here animal was one of our brood mares.'

He stepped closer to run expert hands over the mare, then checked her eyes, mouth and hooves before turning his attention back to Sarah.

'Interested in selling her?' he asked cautiously 'Give you a fair price, if you can show me a bill of sale. If ya can't, I don't want it. Life's complicated enough without me buyin' in stolen horse.'

Sarah shook her head.

'She ain't stolen. I've papers an' everythin', but sorry, no, she ain't for sale.'

Giving her an understanding nod he wiped his forehead on his shirt sleeve then squared off his hat again.

'You got money to pay for her keep?'

She flushed and looked down at her feet. 'Oh yes, money? No, sir, not exactly.'

'No . . . not exactly, now what kind of foolish talk is that supposed to be? If you've no money and no job, how do you expect to live? Folks don't get fat on fresh air and neither do fellas who have a livery to run.'

'I'm a real good worker, honest I am. And I don't give a hoot about the hours. I'll work any time at all. Day or night, it's all the same t' me.'

'You ain't from round here, or I'd know you. If your folks have a stud like you said, why are you all alone in this town, without money or anything else except a horse?'

'My folks, they're both dead. So's my only brother. Him an' me, we were robbed, way up in the mountains back there. Jimmy, he was my kid brother, got himself killed.'

'That's tough luck.' He studied her for a while and pulled at his bottom lip with the side of his finger as he did so. 'You planning on staying or just passing through?'

'I ain't got no kin, so where else should I go?' she shrugged. 'To my way of thinkin' this town is as good as any place else.' Lifting her chin in a gesture of challenge, she stared at him and talked on. 'I've never worked for other folks outside my family before. But like I said, mister, you name it and I can do any mortal thing with horses.'

'Can you read?'

'Uh-huh. Real good.'

Taking out his watch he flipped open the back and held it for her to see close up.

'Tell me what it says on there.'

'Presented to William A. Dawson from John R. Dawson. September 1867.'

'That's fine.' The watch was slipped back into its pocket. 'You write an' do figuring'?'

'Of course. My pa used t' say I could work in a bank.'

'Well, little lady, if you can do chores as good as you work your mouth, you should be able to retire in a few months.' Laughing, he continued his work. 'For the time being, if I take you on as a stable-hand, I won't be paying a fortune,' he warned. 'Business ain't what it used to be before the war. Five dollars a month, three meals a day and any tips the customers care to give ye. Take it or leave it . . . that's the best I can do.'

Sarah's face displayed disappointment; he noticed and frowned.

'Well, that's my best offer. Want the job or not?'

'It's not the money, it's my horse. I don't want to part with her. We've never been parted since the night her momma dropped her.'

'Oh, is that all.' He pointed to an open stall at the far end of the stable. 'Keep the mare in there. If it helps you out any, you can sleep in the hay loft above her. Well, I'm a busy man, so what d' you say, yes or no?'

Her grin told him everything. Momentarily speechless with relief, she nodded violently before she could blurt out her answer.

'Oh, yes! Thanks a heap, mister. When do I start?'

He passed his pitchfork over to her and checked his pocket watch. 'Talkin' about heaps . . .' Taking the reins from her he nodded first at the pile of horse manure and then the wheelbarrow. 'How about right now? Get that done. I'll see to your mare and then rustle up a can of fresh coffee in the office for us.'

★ ★ ★

To Sheriff Craythorn the small town was the same as a hundred others which had mushroomed in the mid West. Outside the saloons some of the work-shy mixed with the old men and laughed at their yarns. Others, bored with their inactivity leaned on the rails of the verandas, or sat on their heels and spat at flies alighting on horse dung deposited near the road edge.

The bank, with polished brass handles on the door and gold lettering on its windows, stood out as a respectable establishment. On the other hand, the livery stable was pure utilitarian, whilst the two-storey hotel and another saloon across the street had the air of false opulence. He had seen them all, almost identical in every respect to a dozen or so other places he had visited.

The joint town jail and sheriff's office was where he had expected to find it, on Main Street. Nearby, a short distance further along, a kid leaned against the red and white striped pole of the barber's shop and played soulful music on his mouth-organ. In the same block, the general store had the day's prices whitewashed all over the window, and its inevitable barrels and boxes of apples and vegetables stacked outside on the freshly swept board-walk.

'I sure don't know what this world is coming to,' he informed his horse, as he dismounted and hitched it to the rail. 'Everywhere you go, every darned thing's the same. Even the folks look and dress like peas in a pod. It's downright confusing.'

The bell suspended on the coiled spring screwed to the back of the law office door bounced and jangled loudly as Craythorn entered.

'Yeah?' growled a belligerent, over-weight man who never even bothered to turn his head to look at Craythorn. Instead, he diligently picked at his teeth with a match while leaning back in the office chair, his heels resting on the desk top. 'You want some-thin'?'

'You the sheriff?' Craythorn asked, dead-pan, taking an instant dislike to the reclining man.

'As good as. I'm the deputy. Why, what ya want?'

Craythorn gave him the dead-eye and made no attempt to cover his contempt for the man.

'Well, I'll tell you: it's the sheriff I want. So get off your ass and fetch him.'

The deputy's lip curled. He stopped picking his teeth.

'Now who the hell . . . ' he began, slowly twisting his head round then caught a glimpse of the star pinned to the newcomer's vest and the way he wore his gunbelt, slung low and tied down.

Craythorn continued to give him the dead-eye.

'You say something . . . *Deputy*?'

The deputy cleared his throat and stood up.

'No sir, the sheriff, he's at the barber's. He has a daily shave there.' Hurrying past he jerked the door open jangling the bell again. 'I'll go get him right away.'

Within a minute, hurrying footsteps sounded outside on the boardwalk. The door burst open and the town sheriff clattered in followed closely by his deputy. Breathing hard from his sudden exertions, he approached Craythorn with his hand extended.

'Jack Jones is the name, I'm the town sheriff. Had the job for nigh on twenty years,' he explained, pumping Craythorn's hand vigorously. 'Yes sir, twenty long peaceful years.'

'Craythorn,' he replied, noticing the panting lawman still had blobs of shaving soap drying in his ears. 'Twenty years? It shows.' He sighed sarcastically, but the other was not bright enough and did not grasp the significance.

'Why thanks, Sheriff, that was a mighty fine thing to say.' He twisted round to his deputy. 'Wasn't it, Wilber?'

Wilber gave a sickly smile and nodded. 'Yeah, Sheriff . . . great.'

'I'm here looking for a girl,' Craythorn butted in before the self-admiration got out of hand. 'She goes by the name of Sarah Handly. It's possible she has a brother, Jimmy, with her, but I doubt it because I have a gut feeling that he may be dead.'

'A girl?' Sheriff Jones looked surprised. 'What she wanted for . . . murder?'

'No, at least not yet. I'd like to find her. I'm concerned about her safety.'

'Well, we don't like troublemakers in this town. No, sir, we don't like 'em at

213

all. What's this girl done?'

'Nothing much. No trouble at all really . . . But she did blow a guy's head clean off his shoulders.'

★ ★ ★

With her natural love of horses, Sarah's new job had turned out to be better than she had expected. At his insistence they had started off on first-name terms but she was always respectful. Bill Dobson was considerate, treated her well and shared out the work fairly between them. This for her was a novelty and more than even her own father had ever done.

The days which followed were long but otherwise happy and some of the events of the recent past began to dim in her mind. Each night she would fall asleep within minutes of snuggling down into her bedroll and not awaken until her boss unbolted and swung open the main doors to let in the morning light.

On one particular night she had fallen asleep as usual only to be woken by noises below. A number of loud-mouthed horsemen argued against the terms of stabling with her boss. Curious, she pressed one eye close to a large knot-hole in one of the loft floorboards and peered down through it. She saw Bill holding a hurricane lamp and horsemen leading their horses, being shown to ready-cleaned empty stalls.

'If you decide to stay three days or more, the charges go down,' her boss emphasized to the night riders. 'The charges are all painted up there on the board outside, clear enough for all to see. Short stays mean more work and expense for us, mucking out and changing the straw after you've gone. It all takes time, and in this business all our workin' time has to be paid for.'

As Sarah blinked away the sleep haze from her eyes somehow the voices were familiar. Then, close to the lamp below and clearly lit by it, a face came into view.

Fright caused an ice-cold tingle of fear to trickle all the way down her spine. She jerked her eye away from the hole, knowing that the slightest movement on her part could disturb chaff or straw ends and cause some bits to fall through cracks in the hayloft floor. Anything falling into the ring of lamplight would easily be seen by those below and give her position away.

'It can't be!' she at last whispered under her breath in disbelief. 'Bart Baxter.' Praying it was all the remnants of a bad dream, a mere figment of her imagination, she pressed her eye again to the knot-hole to make certain, in her heart of hearts knowing she had been correct the first time. 'Those lousy Baxters . . . they're all here!'

'Tell ya what I'll do,' Bart proposed to Bill. 'You can spin a coin and I'll call. We'll toss for it, double or quits for a single day's livery for all the boys an' me.'

216

Grim-faced, Bill Dobson continued to shake his head, adamantly holding to his stated price. 'Mister, I might look like a fool to you, but no sir, I don't hold with gambling, and certainly not where makin' my living is concerned.'

'You're a mighty difficult man to do business with,' Bart Baxter grumbled. 'What's the matter, don't ya like new business?'

'Sure I do. But if you don't like my terms, that's up to you, but they're *my* terms. Everyone else who comes here has been contented. They pay up without question or hassle, now you fellas ride in and want me to change them.'

'We don't want ya to change anythin', mister,' Bart stated, then he grinned. 'We're only lookin' for some flexibility in the deal.'

The livery man stood his ground.

'For the last time, cock your ears and listen good: I'll stick to my prices until all the fires of Hell are snuffed out. If you don't like that, well,' — he waved his arm towards the doorway — 'thanks and goodbye. Get them there animals out of them stalls before they crap on the clean straw then you can move on some place else and see if you get a better deal there.'

14

Jimmy Handly, his limbs still swathed in bandages and held in place by enough wooden splints to build a stockyard fence, sat propped up in his sick-bed by a mountain of feather pillows. At the left of the bed stood the doctor. On the other side, Sailor sat with a troubled expression showing on his sun-browned, wrinkled face.

'So, young-fellow-me-lad,' the old-timer exclaimed, suddenly breaking the silence. 'You're telling us that your memory is still adrift and you're floundering.' Sitting back in the chair he pursued an answer. 'Surely something's come back to ya? Your name, something about your people, and where you used to live? Anything. Your early life can't be a total blank. That last fever you had, it couldn't have ditched everything you ever knew, overboard.'

Before the lad could answer, Sailor turned to the doctor. 'Can it, Doc?'

'Science in the field of medicine has advanced greatly during the last fifty years; however, where the human brain is concerned, we still know very little about its functions,' the medical man confessed. 'When such events as amnesia happen to any one of us, we're in God's hands. Only He can answer your question. I'm afraid all we can do is wait for the broken bones to heal and hope his memory does the same.'

'But I can speak. I understand what you say to me. I know words,' Jimmy persisted. 'I haven't forgotten *them*, have I? I know you and old Sailor, along with other things since I've been conscious after my accident. It's only what happened before then. I can't recall even so much as a glimmer of that, no matter how hard I try.'

'Maybe,' the doctor pointed out quietly, 'you're trying too hard. Learn to relax more. You have youth on your side and the young are resilient, so don't be in such an all-fired hurry. Lie back and rest your mind along with your other injuries, and perhaps your memory will return on its own account.'

'Do as the doc says, son,' Sailor coaxed. 'He's an educated man and education's powerful stuff.'

'Believe me, 'the medic continued, 'I saw this sort of thing happen several times during the war. Men who have been in a really bad way, some not even knowing up from down . . . until some event or other shocked them and brought the entire contents of their minds flooding back to them.' He snapped his fingers. 'Click . . . just as simple as that.'

'Several, eh?' Jimmy mused aloud. 'And what ahout all the other poor devils who *didn't* come out of it?'

'I can't honestly say, because I don't know. I suppose some put it all behind them, went home, got on with living their lives like anyone else. As for the rest, many were bound to go under.

Strange isn't it? Not one of us knows his fate from one day to the next.'

★ ★ ★

Sheriff Craythorn had spent more time in the town than he had originally intended. Apart from giving him the free use of the law-office stables for his stallion and lodgings for himself in one of the unused cells, the town sheriff and his deputies had been useless to him. Although convinced Sarah had arrived at the town ahead of him, he had not laid eyes upon her.

Knowing it was unlikely that the girl would have had enough money to rent a room in the hotel, he systematically began a monotonous questioning routine, going from house to house.

At noon, he retired for a break in the shade offered at one of the saloons. However, his rest period was interrupted by the appearance of the town sheriff who pulled out a chair

222

and joined him uninvited.

'Hi, Craythorn. Not found your little gal yet?' he asked with a smug grin. As he spoke, his arm raised and waved to the barkeep. 'Didn't think ya would,' he went on, taking it for granted he was correct in his assumptions. 'This town's bigger than ya think, and its folks keep to themselves.'

'I've discovered that for myself,' Craythorn admitted. 'Take a look at these knuckles, red-raw through rapping on doors.'

Jack Jones chuckled and lay back in his chair.

'And I bet you didn't get a darned answer ya wanted t' hear.' He broke off as the barkeep placed a bottle and a glass on the table. 'Stick it on my tab, Harry. And fetch another glass for my friend here.'

It was half an hour later when the town sheriff casually broke some unwelcome news to Craythorn.

'Four strangers are in town. From what I've heard they've been asking questions about a certain Sarah Handly and her brother Jimmy.'

Craythorn sat up and took notice. The sheriff went on, 'Folks say that they're acting mighty keen to make their acquaintance with the two youngsters.'

'That'll be Bart Baxter and his three sons,' Craythorn offered.

'Uh-huh . . . came in late last night,' Sheriff Jones agreed. 'According to Bill Dawson, that's the fella over at the livery, he says they were actin' big, tryin' to bully him into lowering his prices.'

'Yeah, that sounds like them. Old man Baxter, he's one of the early breed of go-grab-it rancher who settled on frontier land.'

'Well they sure picked on the wrong man if they thought they'd ride roughshod over Dawson. He's a quiet young fella but he can handle trouble-makers when he needs to.'

* * *

'You hear those fellas causin' a ruckus last night?' Bill Dawson asked Sarah, as together they harnessed a team of trotters to a buggy for the bank manager's wife.

'The noisy galoots woke me. I couldn't help but hear them.'

'You know them?' His question was simple and said as he stared into her eyes.

Caught off guard she flushed at once, averted her eyes and was hesitant in giving him an answer.

'No. Don't think so. Don't forget, it was dark.'

He looked at her sideways, frowning.

'I had a light. You sure you don't know them?'

'Why should I?'

'They know you all right. They asked me straight out if I'd seen you or your brother.'

Sarah's scarlet flush drained from her cheeks.

'What did you tell them?' she almost begged. When he held back, tears came

225

to her eyes and she pleaded with feeling. 'Please Bill, I've got to know. It's important for me to know. *Real important*. To tell the truth, what you said could mean the difference between life and death for me.'

Climbing on to the driving seat, he took the reins in his hand and stared down hard at her for a time, clearly thinking of this latest bombshell of information she had given.

'Please, Bill, please?'

'I'll go deliver this buggy to the bank,' he said coldly, 'and when I come back, I want to see you and a fresh pot of coffee waiting for me in my office. It's high time you an' me had us a talk. An *honest* one!'

With a gentle flick of the reins along the team's backs, he set the horses in motion and without a backward glance drove expertly out of the building. Behind him he left a worried Sarah, ashamed of having lied to him, walking head-down and miserable towards the office in the corner.

★ ★ ★

Bored with enforced inactivity, Jimmy looked out of the window from his bed, watching the passers-by. All at once some noisy cowhands swaggered past the picket fence at the front of the doctor's house. Four abreast on the boardwalk, arrogantly they forced everyone, men and women alike, to step out on to the manure-strewn road and walk around them in order to pass.

Something about their bombastic attitude towards those around them stirred in Jimmy's memory. As they passed by, one of the cow-pokes turned his head to face the window and insolently gazed inside for a brief moment. That simple act was all it took. In that instant Jim Handly's past began to return to him like a flash flood after a quick spring thaw.

'Good heavens above,' exclaimed the doctor's wife who, noticing the rapid change in her patient hurried across the room, to his bedside. 'Are you feeling worse?' she asked, testing the temperature of his brow with her hand. 'Your face, it's turned as white as a bed-sheet. Anyone would think you've seen a ghost. Here, drink some water.'

He took no more than a sip from the glass she held to his lips, looked up at her, and told her what he had discovered. 'I know who I am, ma'am. My name's Jimmy Handly. If she's still alive I have a sister out there somewhere.'

★ ★ ★

Luke Baxter leaned on the saloon bar, scratching at his nose. His features were contorted in deep thought, a sure sign that something troubled him.

'What's wrong, Luke?' his brother Matt asked, puzzled. 'You're kind of quiet, and yer glass is still full. Ya ain't drunk a drop. You sick?'

'Shhh.' Luke half-closed his eyes and then gripped his temples between his

228

over-sized hands. 'I'm a-thinkin'. I've somethin' on my mind.'

Dale overheard and laughed outright.

'Ha! You? Thinkin'? Now that's a truly wondrous thing,' he jeered loud enough for all the men in the saloon to hear. He grinned at his brothers then returned his attention to Luke. 'That somethin' that's balanced on your mind, it must be real small to stay on. At a guess I'd say about half the size of a friggin' cat flea.'

Luke ignored the jibe from his father's favourite. Well used to being the subject of mirth from others, the malicious taunt didn't worry him for as long as spit stayed on a hot pot-bellied stove top.

Sensing an unusual event was occurring, Bart elbowed Matt aside and moved closer to Luke.

'Tell us, what you considerin', boy?'

Again Luke twisted his face, took his hands from his temples and scratched his nose once more.

'Ah think . . . ' he began slowly.

'Yeah, and I think I'm sure . . . I know where a certain person is. Yeah.' He ran his chaw to the other side of his mouth with his tongue. 'Ah could be wrong, but then again, on the other hand . . . '

'For Christs's sake, Luke,' his father exclaimed, 'who in the name of tarnation are yer jawin' on about? Friggin'-well tell me right out.'

Not in the mood to be flustered, Luke spoke quietly with all the dignity at his disposal.

'Jimmy . . . Ah think I see'd him.'

'Jimmy? Jimmy friggin' who?' his exasperated parent demanded.

Luke sensed the moment. Standing to his full height, he faced them and waited, milking his moment of glory for all it was worth. Only when his pa's grinding teeth could be heard, did he nonchalantly hook his thumbs into his gunbelt and make the announcement.

'Jimmy Handly, of course . . . Who else?' The others were standing open-mouthed with dismay as he added for good measure, 'He was inside a house we passed on the way to this saloon.'

'If he was inside,' Dale sneered, 'how come you saw him?'

With a superior grin threatening to push his ears apart, Luke delivered his *coup de grâce*.

'Through a window . . . *stupid*!'

15

'And you're sure that's the whole truth an' nothing but? You ain't been tempted and embroidered it just a little?' The livery owner leaned back in his chair and peered at Sarah over the rim of his coffee mug. 'I don't want you lying to me, not for any reason at all.'

She rose from her chair and leaned on the pine-plank table which stood between them. Her tears had dried and her words were not spoken in anger.

'I ain't lyin' to ya now. But I had no choice before. Bill, I'm sorry, but I was desperate. You were my only hope and I didn't know what else I could do.' When he made no instant reply she blurted out, 'Go fetch a Bible if ya don't believe me. I'll swear to God on it right here and now, that I've been tellin' ya the gospel truth.'

Bill made no comment but continued to rock his chair and without blinking looked her in the eyes.

Defiant, her own eyes returned his gaze.

'I don't know what else I can say, except you've been real good to me since I rode in here. Giving me this job, a place to sleep an' everythin'. I won't ever lie to you again. I promise. But I know trust is a very special thing and if ya want me to go . . . well . . . ' She shrugged apologetically. 'I'll understand.'

The empty coffee mug banged down on the table and he stood up with such violence that his chair fell over backwards with a clatter.

'Go? I don't want you to go.' Then, realizing he had yelled at her he lowered his voice. 'Sarah, that's the last thing I want. If you shot and killed those two men like you said, I'm sure you had the best of reasons in mind when you did it.'

'*If*?' Disbelief and disappointment showed clearly in her single word. 'You still think I've lied.'

'No! No, I don't, it's just that I'm putting things kind of badly.' He walked around the table and grasped her gently by her elbows. 'Can't you tell? What I'm really trying to say is . . . I *want* you to stay . . . I *need* you to stay. And Sarah, I guarantee that ain't a lie, neither.'

* * *

Hurrying feet, feet with light steps paused outside the sheriff's office, then, without knocking, the doctor's wife burst in.

'Sheriff, my husband needs you to come over to our place and bring some guns with you.'

The town sheriff exchanged puzzled looks with Craythorn who had perched one thigh on the end of the desk.

'Guns, what do we need guns for?'

'Hurry, man, and bring your deputy and this other gentleman if he's willing to help.' She had already retreated to the door and was leaving. 'No time to explain, just get there, or there's likely to be a killing.' With that she was gone, her footsteps retiring along the boardwalk.

'Come on, Craythorn, you heard the lady,' Jack Jones called, reaching for his gunbelt and buckling it. 'And you bring the scattergun and spare shells,' he ordered his deputy. 'The office can look out for itself.'

They caught up with the lady and she waved them on with a shouted warning. 'Go round the back. The porch door is open and you're expected.'

'Bossy woman,' Craythorn remarked. 'Who is she?'

'The doc's wife. Has a twenty-two carat heart of gold.'

Reaching the rear of the house without incident, they entered as directed, their guns already drawn and ready to fire.

'Ah,' the doctor greeted them. 'Reinforcements, good! My patient will be relieved. He tells me there are four of them liable to kill him at any moment.'

'Where are these desperadoes, Doc?' Jack Jones asked, as carefully he and Craythorn eased past the medic. 'Out front are they?'

'Oh, no, they're not here yet. But they will be. My patient is confident of it.'

Both lawmen stopped dead in their tracks, looked at each other then holstered their pistols.

'This patient of yours,' groaned the confused town sheriff, 'he some sort of lunatic? Are you sure he knows what he's saying?'

'Come through and see for yourself. The lad's in this room here.'

At first, because of the remaining bruises and a surgical dressing on the boy's face, Craythorn did not recognize the patient in the bed.

'Sheriff, where did you spring from? Mister Craythorn, am I glad t' see you.'

'Jimmy? Good God almighty, I had an idea you were already dead somewhere.'

Jack Jones coughed and cleared his throat.

'Is this conversation strictly private, or is somebody around here ready to let me in on the deal?'

'Meet Jimmy Handly, Sheriff,' said the doctor. 'The luckiest man alive.'

The sheriff scratched the back of his neck.

'Handly? Mmm . . . Handly, yeah. I have an idea I've recently heard all about yer sister, son.'

'There are four rough-looking men coming this way,' the doctor's breathless wife called from behind the bedroom doorway. 'And they've all got guns out and ready.'

★ ★ ★

237

'This the house?' With drink in his belly, Bart Baxter was in no mood to wait and plan an execution. His boy was dead and Handly was going to pay for it.

'That's the one, Pa.' Luke gloried in his new status as temporary adviser to his father. 'That window there. He's in the bed.'

'Bed? Ya didn't mention no dang bed.' Bart's confidence waned as someone levelling a Colt at him stepped out from the corner of the house and yelled, 'Stop right there, Baxter. Drop your gun and tell your boys to follow suit.'

'Craythorn,' Bart snarled, baring his teeth. 'I might've guessed it would be you pokin' yer nose in my business again. But ya don't impress me none. Your badge ain't worth chicken shit in this town.'

'Maybe not,' called Jack Jones's voice from the other corner of the house, 'but mine sure as hell is. Now do as the man says. All of ya, drop 'em, and

I ain't waitin' for a count of three neither.'

As chance would have it, in those split seconds of indecision, the deputy turned up on the scene brandishing the twelve-gauge. Full of self-importance and with more guts than brains, he stepped over the picket fence and backed until he stood between Craythorn and the Baxters.

'All right, Sheriff, I've got 'em quakin' in their boots.'

Luke, his head still bursting with notions of grandeur, decided to push his luck one more time and go for broke. Squeezing the trigger as he spun round he fired his .45 and drilled the smug deputy through the chest at point blank range.

The shot acted as a catalyst upon the rest of Luke's family. Each, taking his chance, ran ducking and weaving for cover while blazing snap-shots at the lawmen.

Craythorn, who had had the sense to duck back round the corner, saw to his horror the deputy fire the shotgun during his death throes. By accident, both barrels discharged their loads in the direction of Jack Jones.

The town sheriff seemed surprised. He let his Colt Peacemaker spin lazily on his finger then slip unfired from his hand, and stared down at the scarlet flower spreading across the chest of his shirt. Then a Baxter bullet slammed into him driving him back against the house wall. Sliding sideways, he collapsed with his face in a clump of flowers, leaving behind an arc of his life-blood staining the white painted wood.

'I think ya were right, Luke,' Bart admitted, as he shared the cover offered by a horse trough. 'If the Handly kid wasn't inside, I don't think the law would've been there protectin' him from us.' He paused. 'Ya told us the boy was in bed, so he must be sick or hurt.'

'That's right, Pa. I wouldn't tell you no lies.'

'There's only that Craythorn guy agin us,' Dale shouted from a doorway. 'Ya want us to rush him while you go after Handly?'

'I'll fix Handly for ya, Pa. Then you an' the boys can draw Craythorn's fire and make a run for the horses.'

Bart looked with affection at Luke.

'Ya know, son, I've had you figured all wrong. You've been foolin' us all these years, makin' out you're stupid, when you ain't. I'm proud of you, boy.'

Luke's ego blossomed.

'Let me finish Jimmy Handly, will ya, Pa?'

'Ya think you can do it?'

'Shot that shotgun-totin' deputy, didn't I?

'So ya did, son, so ya did. Fixed him real good.' He smiled and nodded. 'Yer want to do it, you do it. Get ready to go when I give you the word. In the mean time, I'm goin' to organize us some protection for when we shoot the shit out of that jumped-up lawman.'

* * *

Sheriff Mark Craythorn, unseen by the Baxters, had entered the house through the porch at the rear. While the doctor and his wife moved their patient to the safety of another room, he hid by the curtain side of the sickroom window.

He had watched the besiegers moving from cover to cover, but as he was out-gunned, did not waste any ammunition at such awkward and distant targets.

Fresh movement drew his attention to a horse trough. Not long after, Bart Baxter made a surprisingly fast run for such a big man, and made the safety of some buildings further away from the doctor's house.

'Now then, I wonder what scheme you're working on, Baxter,' Craythorn mused. 'One thing is certain, it surely ain't for my benefit.'

The doctor came and poked his head around the doorway.

'Anything happening?'

'Not yet, Doc, but it will, and soon,

so keep your head down real close to the ground.' An idea came to him. 'I don't suppose you have a gun I can borrow?'

The medic shook his head.

'Sorry, but no. Your job's different to mine. I was only trained to save life, so I've never felt the need for one.'

'It's a pity. If they rush us and I don't make every shot count, you might find that need mighty soon.'

* * *

'There's been no more firing. Maybe it's all over,' Sarah said hopefully, clambering up the fixed vertical ladder to the hayloft. 'I'm goin' to take me a look-see, out of the loadin' door.'

'No use,' Bill Dobson explained. 'Your sight's blocked off in that direction by the door when it opens, so you might as well come down here with me.'

Sarah had disappeared from view. After a minute or so, he grew curious.

'Sarah?'

'Yeah, what?'

'What you doing?'

'Getting us a little more protection in case them Baxters are at the bottom of that shootin' out there.' She appeared at the top of the ladder and gingerly climbed down with her shotgun hung round her neck by twine.

'Sarah, there's no need for that. This is my place and I'll supply all the protection it needs.' When she reached the ground he made a grab for her gun but she was too quick and snatched it out of his way and held it close to her body.

'No need, eh? Well, all I can say, Bill, is you don't know the Baxters. If they find me, they'll hang me. It's true. Then, likely as not, they'll string you up to dangle alongside me.' She patted her twelve-gauge. 'That ain't goin' to happen to either one of us, because I won't let it.'

★ ★ ★

244

Sailor rode along Main Street on his mule and wondered why the town was so deserted. A hundred yards from the doctor's house he noticed some cowpokes loading up a flat-top wagon so that all the boxes and sacks were stacked on one side instead of balanced across it. Something was not right. A wagon was never built to lean over so much.

The men worked too hurriedly and were constantly looking furtively about them. When he passed them by, a couple placed their hands on their gun butts, but he heard the oldest man with them warn them, 'No. He's only a prospector, likely comin' in for some red-eye or bacca. He won't bother us.'

Turning the mule by the white house, he saw what looked like a pile of rags had been dumped over the garden fence. However, as he drew closer it became clear that the bundle was the body of a man. Beside the cadaver's outstretched arm lay a shotgun.

Wild yells of 'Yee-ha' and 'Ya-hoo, ya, ya', were quickly followed by the rumble of cartwheels and the drumming of hooves. Turning his head, he saw the oddly loaded and apparently driverless cart at speed behind him and drawing closer. It half swung round as it skidded to a stop. Then guns were firing. Bullets zinged past and punched holes into the wooden walls close to the corner. A man arose from behind a water trough and hared for the garden, leapt the fence and made for the window where Jimmy was. The man held a gun and was about to use it.

'Hey, you,' Sailor shouted, fearing for his young friend. 'Stop or I'll fire,' he threatened, dragging at his own gun in desperation.

Before the weapon was drawn free of its holster, Luke fired and knocked him clean off the back of the mule. Then, laughing like a maniac, just for the hell of it, he fired several shots into the animal before returning his attention back to the window.

Elated, Luke looked through the glass, searching for his intended target. The bed was empty, his target had gone . . . But Craythorn was not. The lawman stood still while the pistol was aimed at him and the trigger squeezed. Once . . . click. Twice . . . another click.

'You didn't count your bullets, fella, but I did,' Craythorn said. The Colt in the sheriff's fist jerked twice. The window shattered and a myriad slivers of glass skewered Luke's eyes and cheeks. At about the same instant, the heavy lead bullets hammered in the front of his skull and then carried on out of the back to liberally splatter sticky particles of brain among the flowers.

'Some bastard got Luke,' Craythorn heard shouted from a man on the cart. He raised the Colt again and fired a single round through the broken pane. 'And I got you too, fella,' he muttered with some satisfaction. 'That's for the old-timer.'

'Now he's gone and killed Matt,' another Baxter yelled. 'Come on, let's get out of here, we ain't gonna do any good for them even if we stay.'

★ ★ ★

Soon after the second lot of firing had died, Sarah and Bill listened to a cart being driven at the gallop until it was hauled and braked to a stop in front of the livery.

'It's them. I recognize the voices,' Bill whispered.

'Yeah, me too,' Sarah whispered back as the main doors were opened from outside to swing wide on well-greased hinge pins. 'Seems they've taken a lickin' from whoever was shootin'. There's only two of them there.'

Their weapons held cocked and ready, Bart Baxter and his only remaining son walked in cautiously, their heads moving from side to side looking for danger signs.

'You go saddle up while I stand

guard an' figure out how to make sure the folks in this no-good town remember us Baxters for a long time.'

Bill made to stand up from behind a partition. Sarah grabbed him and hauled him back.

'What in hell's name did ya think ya was gonna do,' she hissed angrily, 'commit suicide?'

'I could hold them 'til the law gets here. It's my civic duty.'

'Duty, my butt. All ya'd do is get yourself killed.'

'And you'd care?' he asked, and waited for her answer.

'Shh! Bart's comin' this way. Looks suspicious. Get ready just in case he makes a play for it.'

'What's he doing now?'

'He's stopped by the clean straw store.' She stopped whispering and watched for a while.

'Well, what's happening? Can you still see him?'

'Yes ... Oh my Lord, he's lit a lantern. I think he's ... yes he is, he's aimin' to drop it in the straw.'

Before Bill could make a move she had stood up and swung her shotgun to her shoulder.

'Bart Baxter, drop that lamp and you're dead.'

'And if that son of yours tries to make a move,' Bill joined in, 'he'll be able to whistle through the back of his head.'

Dale at the far end of the building weighed the odds and decided to risk the livery man's lack of shooting practice. In a blur of motion he ducked below the partition as Bill fired. Too late, the bullet buried itself in a wooden post close to where Dale's head had been.

'You hold tight, I'll get the both of 'em, Pa.'

'The hell ya will; I want one of them,' his father retorted, dropping the lamp on to the straw and at the same time taking a shot at Sarah.

He was not given the opportunity of a second attempt. She side-stepped from the protection of the partition and snapped off a shot as coolly as if he was a jack-rabbit destined for the pot. Blasted with buck-shot as the others had been, his massive body was driven back to fall among the blazing straw.

'Pa,' screamed the last of the Baxter clan, leaving cover to blaze away with his revolver. 'I'll get them. I'll get them good for ya.'

It proved to be an empty boast. Bill Dawson was a better shot than he thought and left a bullet deep inside Dale's chest. Shocked at his success he stood dumbly watching as the dying man staggered a few faltering paces and struggled to line the sights of his pistol and shoot.

A shot rang out, echoing through the length of the livery building. It was all over, Dale, flung back by the impact of a second bullet now lay spread-eagled and statue-still, his eyes already dulling.

'You darned fool,' Craythorn exclaimed, as he walked towards the shocked owner of the livery. Holstering his Colt he asked, 'You want to be killed by a man already as good as dead?' He thumbed at the burning straw. 'Better attend to that fire while I let the horses out into the corral before they all go loco.'

For the first time Bill noticed the neighing and stamping of the animals in the stalls. He felt as though he was in a horrible dream, rooted to the spot and unable to get his brain working.

As he began to drive the first of the horses from the building, Craythorn casually called out, 'Oh, by the way, I heard a shotgun go off. Does it happen to belong to a girl called Sarah?'

'A girl? Sarah!' In a panic, Bill turned and dashed to where he'd last seen her. He found her in a stall. She lay face down without any sign of movement and with blood trickling from her hair and staining the straw bright red. He felt numb, as though his whole world had suddenly come to an end.

He knew people were moving about. Buckets rattled and clanged. Water splashed and he smelled steam mixed with the smoke from the fire but he did not care, he stood in anguish, his eyes fixed on Sarah.

'Out of the way man.' Someone pushed him aside and knelt down beside Sarah. It was the doctor who was already taking her pulse with one hand as his other felt among her hair. When he brought this hand away, his fingers were covered in blood. The doc looked up at Bill and smiled reassuringly. 'Well, don't be so glum. It's only a bit of a scalp wound. A bullet's knocked her out from behind, that's all. She'll be fine in no time.'

* * *

By the time Sarah came back to consciousness, the fire had been dealt with by the townsfolk and the horses returned to their stalls. With Bill's arm to support her they walked accompanied by Craythorn and the doctor.

'You taking me to jail?' she asked outright.

'Why should I?' Sheriff Craythorn grinned. 'As far as I know you've never done anything to deserve it.'

'You're going to spend a night or two at my house,' the doc explained, 'just as a precaution and to get a couple of stitches in that wound.'

'I almost forgot.' Craythorn winked at her knowingly. 'There's a surprise waiting for you at the doc's. I have a feeling you know him.'

THE END

McKINNEY'S REVENGE

Mike Stotter

When ranch-hand Thadius McKinney finds his newly-wedded wife in the arms of his boss, the powerful, land-hungry Aaron Wyatt, something inside him snaps. Two gunblasts later, McKinney is forced to flee into the night with the beef-baron's thugs hot on his trail, baying for his blood. A man cannot run forever, and even when his back-trail is littered with bodies, the fighting isn't over. McKinney decides it is time for Wyatt to pay the Devil.

THE BROTHERS DEATH

Bill Wade

Russ Hartmann was a wandering cowboy who had seen better days. Two riders followed him out of the past: one brought good news, the other brought murder and disaster. When the Brothers Death took a hand, it appeared certain that Hartmann would go under. But a ranching lady coveted his skill with a gun, and he went to work for her. Slowly he dug both Evelyn Cross's Broken C and himself out of trouble — but he kept the undertaker busy in the process.

RHONE

James Gordon White

Former bounty hunter Phil Rhone finds himself in a mess of trouble when he agrees to help Brad Miller to find his abducted wife, Lorna. They team up with Susan Prescott, a blonde beauty seeking the killers of her family. The hunt takes them up into the isolated mountains to a slave labour gold mine, where they confront sadistic Nelson Forbes. The odds are against them, but Susan thirsts for revenge and Miller isn't leaving without his wife . . .